LAVENDER

Annemarieke Tazelaar

ISBN:13: 978-1479189786
ISBN 10:1479189782

DEDICATION

This book is dedicated to friends in my writing groups – in Renton, Washington and in Des Moines, Washington, who helped me to edit the manuscript and suggest various ways of fine-honing the story.

CHAPTER ONE

Ever since she could remember, one particular relative filled Tivoli Hansen with a mixture of awe and curiosity.

Aunt Evelyn.

Aunt Evelyn never attended family picnics or holiday dinners. She was absent from weddings and funerals.

And yet, they all felt her presence.

Each year, at the annual Fourth of July family picnic, a blue 1949 Ford station wagon with wooden sides swept into the parking lot of Clearwater Village Park on the Tennessee River. While Tivoli and everyone else stared at the vintage car that looked as though it had just escaped from the Ford Motor Museum, Aunt Evelyn's servant, Gerard, unfolded himself from the driver's seat, opened the hatch, and lifted out a large wicker basket. Then, with energy that belied his seventy-some years, the wiry, white-haired man strode toward the gathering of the Hansens, the O'Learys, and the Jacksons.

Tivoli's granddad Hansen always invited Gerard to join them. Gerard would smile politely and decline the offer, and then back out the shiny wagon and speed away.

On an afternoon before every Christmas, he would show up in the Ford at the home of Tivoli's grandparents and unload shopping bags containing books wrapped in lavender paper and tied with purple ribbons.

The Christmas before Tivoli turned thirteen, relatives arrived and added their gifts to the mountain of presents under the tree. As the day progressed, people opened their new treasures.

Unwrapping Aunt Evelyn's gifts, however, was a shared ritual after the family meal. One by one, each person chose an unlabeled package. Grandma Hansen, Aunt Evelyn's only sister, opened hers first. A musty odor wafted from the cloth-bound book as she held up her gift: "*The Taming of the Shrew,*" she said. "I wonder how many Shakespeare volumes she has left? Seems like each year she gives away half a dozen." She looked inside the book cover. "No inscription."

An uncle unwrapped *For Whom the Bell Tolls*, and read, "'To the stunning Evelyn: may your life be filled with the beauty you radiate!' Signed by none other than Ernest Hemingway!"

Grandma Hansen sighed. "My sister was such a beauty in her youth. Tall, with dark auburn hair, a few light freckles on her face in the summer, large blue eyes and the smallest nose in the family. Men flocked around her, hanging on to her every witty word."

Most of the books – *The Adventures of Huckleberry Finn, Moll Flanders, Tom Jones, Windswept, A Gift from the Sea,* had apparently been given to Aunt Evelyn by one person: Morris.

Tivoli watched and listened while each person read Morris' sentiments. Her brother, cousins, and uncles mumbled the words with embarrassed grins. One aunt dabbed her eyes with a handkerchief.

"To Evelyn – My heart will long for you always – your devoted Morris."

"To Evelyn – how wonderful it might have been – you and I. Your wistful admirer, Morris."

"To my darling Evelyn: If only I could take you away from your secret life and show you the wide, wide world! Morris."

"This is too weird," said Robert, Tivoli's twelve-year-old cousin. "I heard she's just a dried up old prune."

"Hush!" his mother admonished.

"Can't blame the boy for those words, Sondra," said Tivoli's father. "For most of her eighty years, she's been sitting in that dark, gloomy house day after day, shades drawn, never stepping outside to breathe fresh air and feel the sun on her face!"

Grandma said, "You'd never guess we're sisters. I go there for an hour once a year, on her birthday. It's so stuffy and dreary in the parlor where she always sits when I arrive, that I can hardly breathe, and after the first ten minutes, we have absolutely nothing to say to each other."

Tivoli had heard this conversation every year at the Christmas gathering, but this time, she paid more attention. She knew that she would be invited to visit the elderly aunt, as all her girl cousins had, when she turned thirteen the following November.

"What about the rest of the house, Grandma?" she asked.

"Not nearly as dismal. Gerard airs the place out regularly and opens the drapes and shades. Says he would like to paint the outside, but she won't let him. We don't know why. Maybe she doesn't want the house to attract attention."

But it was Morris who Tivoli couldn't get out of her mind, and later that day, she sought out her grandmother. "Tell me about Morris, Grandma."

"Very sad. They were so in love. Then he was drafted into the Army, and I remember them arguing. She begged him to find a way to avoid the service, but he wanted to serve his country. By the time Morris' unit shipped overseas to Europe in early 1944, their relationship had been over for a year. He was killed in action, somewhere in France."

"How awful!"

Grandma wiped her hands and sat down on the couch. "We all knew she was heartbroken. She had inherited the old house by this time, so she moved in and, as far as any of us know, has never left."

"What does she do all day?"

That's a mystery to me. I do know she reads a lot and watches television. Loves music, especially British composers. She looks trim enough; her face has a rosy glow and isn't near as wrinkled as mine. She doesn't seem unhappy or cranky. She lives, as near as I can figure, in a world all her own."

That winter, whenever she rode with her parents, Tivoli asked if they could drive past Hickory Manor. One Saturday, she walked the three miles to Aunt Evelyn's to be alone with her thoughts. Surrounded by snow, the mansion stood stark and lonely at the end of a long driveway. Tivoli shivered as she stared at the dark, paint-hungry house that reminded her of a haunted house in a Halloween movie cartoon. A single light shone from behind a draped window to the left of the front door. Was that where Aunt Evelyn sat all day?

She walked home, kicking clumps of snow with thread-bare boots and gliding over patches of ice. Why, she wondered, did Aunt Evelyn want to meet her grandnieces when they turned thirteen? What did she talk about? And what would Tivoli say to her great-aunt? Should she ask her about her health? Should she show an interest in the house? She imagined herself in that mysterious room with the lone light. Would she be scared? And what about Gerard? Would he be there, too? She hoped so. He would be a comforting presence.

In the spring, her soccer team began practice, and, busy with band rehearsals and homework, Tivoli had little time to think about Aunt Evelyn, let alone wander past the foreboding house.

In early August, Tivoli attended the wedding of her cousin, Carolyn, and as expected, Gerard brought a gift wrapped in hues of purple – a coffee samovar. In the past, Aunt Evelyn had given crystal bowls, pewter plates, crocheted table cloths – all heirlooms from Hickory Manor.

Summer camp and swimming lessons crowded the rest of Tivoli's vacation, and the bustle of new classes and friends took up the beginning of the school year.

By November, Tivoli anticipated her thirteenth birthday with excitement mixed with dread. Now just weeks away, the date was already set for her visit with Aunt Evelyn. The O'Leary twins, who survived this ordeal eight months earlier, filled her in with the details of their visit.

"It's dark and spooky in there. We had to sit on a velvet couch that stunk like moth balls," Judith said.

Jeanne continued, "Gerard brought in a silver tray with a tea pot and stupid little cups. And rum balls, made with real rum!"

"What does she look like?"

The twins spoke in turns, each adding a sentence, as though the conversation had been worked out between them. Judith took the lead. "She's tall. Bunch of gray hair on top of her head."

"Weird black shoes with laces," Jeanne added.

"And she smells like a flower. Lavender, probably."

"What did she talk about?" asked Tivoli.

"She asked about school. Wanted to know what we plan to be when we grow up."

"Yeah, and she asked if we had boyfriends! We told her we both liked the same boy, Bobby Slape. But he likes Hennie."

"Then what did she say?"

Jeanne glanced at her sister. "Laughed. Said that Bobby is a lucky boy, because three women wanted him."

"What was so bad about the visit? She sounds all right."

Judith's voice dropped to a conspiratorial whisper. "It's the place itself – that house, her stuffy, dark room."

"And that wall!" added Jeanne. "Wait 'til you see *the wall.* It gave me the creeps!"

"Wall? What are you talking about?"

The twins cast knowing glances at each other. "You'll find out," said Judith.

Jeanne frowned, "And you're the next victim!"

"What! Tell me now! Otherwise, I won't go."

Judith lowered her voice to a whisper. "It's alive!"

"The wall? What do you mean, it's alive?"

Jeanne wagged a finger at Tivoli and sing-songed, "If you don't go, you'll never know."

After they left, Tivoli walked to the old mansion once again. Where was this wall? Why did she have to go? Why did she have to follow this tradition? Couldn't she get out of it?

That evening, Tivoli sank next to her father on the couch and asked him about her aunt.

He laid down the Sports section of *The Tennessean* and put his arm on the backrest. "Aunt Evelyn is getting on in years. When she was young, perhaps twenty, she inherited the house from her great aunt, Cora O'Leary. Cora's life was very much like that of Aunt Evelyn, a single lady who never left the house."

"Why not, Dad?"

"She didn't have to. All her needs were met with enough inheritance to pay the bills. She had a servant like Gerard, someone who looked a lot like him."

"How did Cora get the house?"

Tivoli's father cleared his throat. "That's the truly strange thing. She also inherited it from a great aunt. That lady was named Martha."

"An O'Leary?"

"No, Jackson, daughter of Ira Jackson, also Irish. Martha's father built the house on the River in 1830 and named it Hickory Manor. He had fought against the British in 1815, right alongside of Andrew Jackson, who became President just when Ira began to build the house."

"So are we related to a *president*?" asked Tivoli.

"Probably not. There is no evidence of it. But Ira was proud of his name. All the children married except Martha, so she inherited the house."

Tivoli clasped her hands and stretched her arms. "What does this have to do with me, or Judith and Jeanne, or the other cousins?"

Her father picked up his cup from the coffee table. "We think Evelyn's looking for the right person to inherit her house."

"Who'd want to live the life of a hermit?"

"I'm sure that's not a requirement. No reason why the new owner shouldn't marry and bring up her family in the house, or renovate and sell."

"I feel sorry for her, Dad. She must be a pretty lonely old woman. Bored, too."

"No one has ever heard her complain, or even seen her grumpy. But none of us really know her, either. She's the great mystery of the family."

Tivoli shivered. "I'm scared to meet her. And I sure don't want that house! Do I really have to go?"

Her father peered over his reading glasses and raised an eyebrow. "You don't have to go, honey. Your mother and I don't care, one way or another. It's totally up to you. But all of your cousins who have made their coming-of-age visit have survived," he said, smiling.

Her father had given her a choice, and now that she had an option, Tivoli knew that she would not refuse. She had to go inside that dreary house. She had to see the eerie wall.

She *had* to meet Aunt Evelyn.

CHAPTER TWO

On the morning after her thirteenth birthday, Tivoli dressed quickly, fumbling with the buttons on the new blue dress her mother had made and hurried downstairs, where her father waited to drive her to the fortress-like mansion.

The house stood several hundred feet back from the road, and the driveway, which curved to the front door, was flanked on either side by the gray stalks of dormant lavender bushes.

As she stepped out of the car, Tivoli yearned to ask her father to go in with her and wait somewhere in the house, but she felt she needed to do this alone. She took a deep breath and started up the winding cobblestone path.

As Tivoli approached, the stones that made up the wall of the first floor looked even more foreboding and dark than they did from the road. Tivoli grasped an iron rail as she climbed the six chipped and peeling wooden steps to the porch. The massive wood door loomed before her. When she reached for the brass anchor-shaped knocker, it fell back with an echo that reverberated from within the house. She waited, her heart pounding.

The door swung open, and to her relief, she stared up into Gerard's friendly face.

"Come in, Miss Hansen!" he said, a musical lilt in his voice. "Your Aunt has been anticipating your visit. May I take your coat?"

"I…I would like to keep it on," Tivoli stammered.

"Why, that's quite all right, but you'll find the room quite comfortable."

She followed Gerard down a long hallway with windows revealing a courtyard along one side. Shafts of late autumn sun shone into the hall, and Tivoli felt its warmth. At the end, they faced another door. Gerard turned the handle and looked back at Tivoli. "Wait here, Miss, and I will announce you."

She could hear orchestral music drifting from the room. She recognized a melody she had heard at Grandma Hansen's. The music stopped, and too soon, Gerard returned, holding the door for her to enter. She walked in cautiously, and the gloomy darkness startled her. Near a window draped with ivory-colored lace, a tall woman rose from a chair. She leaned on a cane and limped slightly as she walked toward the girl and stretched out her hand to clasp Tivoli's. Tivoli stared into clear gray-blue eyes behind steel-rimmed glasses.

"Welcome to my home, Tivoli. My goodness, you're just a slip of a girl. You don't take much after your father. Peter is such a giant."

"Yes, ma'am." Tivoli was aware that her voice was barely audible.

"Aunt Evelyn, if you please, child. I like the sound of that much better. Won't you sit down?" She waved her arm toward a maroon velvet couch.

"Thank you, Aunt Evelyn." As Tivoli sank into the soft cushions of the sofa, the odor of camphor wafted into the air.

"Let me look at you, dear. Hmm. Straight honey-blonde hair, from your mother's side. Hazel eyes. Clear skin. Not a Hansen look, but quite lovely, all the same!"

Tivoli blushed and looked down at her feet. She felt on display, as if she were a horse at a county fair.

Aunt Evelyn retreated to her chair and rang a bell. Soon, Gerard appeared, wheeling a cart that held a tray with a teapot and two fragile cups, and tiny spoons, tongs, and sugar cubes on a silver dish. Another plate displayed round-shaped pastry, covered with powdered sugar. He placed the cart next to Aunt Evelyn and left the room.

Tivoli's eyes adjusted as she surveyed her surroundings. Heavy purple drapes framed the lace curtains, and a built-in bookcase towered behind her aunt's chair. Aunt Evelyn sat very straight, a light gray blouse tucked into a navy skirt, a blue cardigan draped over her shoulders. Her steel-gray hair was pulled away from her face and tied behind her head in a French roll, adorned with an amber-colored comb.

When Tivoli turned, a huge bucolic landscape caught her eye. The painting covered a whole wall. When she looked up at Aunt Evelyn, she noticed the woman watching her with studious concentration.

"What do you see, child?" she asked.

"J-just looking," stammered Tivoli. "I've never been in such a fancy room before."

"Oh, I'm sure you live in a lovely home." Aunt Evelyn turned to the cart.

"Can I help?" Tivoli asked, rising from the couch.

"Why, thank you," the woman answered. "They don't usually ask, my grandnieces. So many of them. You're number sixteen."

Tivoli picked up the pot and poured the tea. "I'm not the last one. You'll be seeing a whole lot more Hansens, O'Learys, and Jacksons. Auntie Beverly is expecting a baby in February. It's gonna be a girl."

"*Going to be*, young lady. Well, that's news. I won't be around for another fifteen years, though, I'm sure."

"Oh, but ma'am, I mean Aunt, I'm sure you will. Everyone says you're far too…" Tivoli stopped in mid-sentence.

"Too what, Tivoli? Speak up, child."

"Oh, nothing."

To Tivoli's surprise, the elderly woman laughed. "Too ornery to die? I'll bet that's what they say. 'When's the old biddy going to kick the bucket?'"

The remark seemed uncharacteristic, coming from the staid, proper woman, and Tivoli blubbered, "N…no, Aunt! I've never heard anybody say that!"

"Well, I wouldn't blame them if they did. One lump or two?"

"What? Oh, the sugar. Two, I think. I don't know. I've never tasted tea before."

"So what do you drink? Milk, probably. Or that sweet green beverage I see advertised on TV. I asked Gerard to get me some one time. Vile taste."

Tivoli returned to her seat, placing the tea on a table beside her. Her eyes wandered back to the painting, and she shivered. The pastoral scene seemed to quiver, as if a wind stirred the trees. In the far left corner, a vivid patch of purple flowers appeared newly-painted.

Evelyn O'Leary observed the girl's gaze. "Martha, one of your ancestors, fancied herself a painter. She had talent, but she always copied the works of one particular artist."

"Why? Who was it?"

"An Englishman, William Turner. And why? Well, child, if you are curious enough to visit me again some time, I will tell you more about her. Her paintings hang throughout the house, and her letters lie in a small trunk." She looked up. "Would you like a rum ball, Tivoli?"

"Yes'm, thank you, Aunt Evelyn."

"What do you like most about school?"

Tivoli had anticipated the question. "This year, I like history."

"My favorite subject, too. Just why do you like it?"

"My teacher comes in as a different person every day. Once, he dressed as George Washington, trying to get across the Delaware. The next day, he came in as Paul Revere, pretending to ride a horse, and saying, 'One if by land, and two if by sea.' We're up to the Civil War now, and last week he was Abraham Lincoln, wearing a stovepipe hat and a beard. Looked just like him. And he recited the *Gettysburg Address*. We have to memorize it, but it's not so hard, because it really makes sense to me now."

"Well, dear, never forget that piece of oratory, and try to learn *Paul Revere's Ride,* as well. I did many years ago, as well as other great poetry, and being able to recite these pieces of literature, can help you through tough times."

Aunt Evelyn pointed to an ornately carved wooden box on a shelf underneath the windowsill. "Bring that here, young lady, and put it on the table next to me."

Tivoli did as ordered, glancing again at the mural. From this angle, the trees beyond the field looked taller, darker. Her aunt pulled out a chain that hung around her neck. Several keys emerged from under her blouse. She chose a small brass one and unlocked the box.

"This is especially for your eyes, young Tivoli. For many years, no one has seen the contents of this box except me. But I feel that you, of all my nieces, will be interested in what I have to show you."

Tivoli stared at the strange wall as the elderly woman riffled through papers and pulled out a brittle, yellowed envelope. She opened it and took out several black and white photographs.

"I had a teacher much like yours. He also acted out historical characters from classic books that he adapted into plays. This picture is from a scene in *A Tale of Two Cities*." She pointed to a slender girl with luxuriant dark hair. "That is your old Aunt. I played the part of Lucy. And this boy played the hero, Charles Darnay."

"Who was he in real life?" Tivoli asked, staring at the handsome, dark-haired boy in the picture.

The old woman hesitated, clearing her throat. "His name is Morris."

When Gerard escorted her out of the room, Tivoli had to squint in the bright sunlight that flooded the hallway. As he led her to the front door, he said, smiling, "I hope you enjoyed your visit, Miss!"

"Yes, I did, Mr...."

"Just Gerard. It's my only name."

"I enjoyed my aunt very much, Gerard! She asked me to come visit again."

"That's a real honor, Miss. She doesn't often extend that invitation." He pulled out a card. "Here's my phone number. Next time you wish to visit Hickory Manor, just give me a call. I'm almost always here, and I will arrange a time with Miss O'Leary."

She looked at the card. *Gerard – 615 527-8900.*

Tivoli started down the long path between the lavender bushes. Glancing back, she found the room she had stared at so many times in the past months. The heavy curtain was pulled back slightly, and, although she couldn't see her aunt, she guessed the elderly woman was watching her, so she waved and smiled. She walked slowly to her father's car at the bottom of the drive, thinking about the visit and about Aunt Evelyn's comment.

His name is Morris. Not *was,* but *is.* Her aunt spoke proper English and would not have made such a mistake. Tivoli remembered the Christmas gift books and the inscription: *Morris*. She thought about Aunt Evelyn's smile when she said his name, a smile and a certain glow that had made her seem younger, more vibrant.

What would she tell her mother? Grandma? The twins? Just that she thought Aunt Evelyn was a nice lady, and the visit had been pleasant. But in her heart, she felt excited and eager to learn more about her aunt. And she wanted to know about that wall. It had to be more than a mere painting, she was sure.

CHAPTER THREE

A week passed before Tivoli called Gerard. She had wavered over the decision she could not get out of her mind, Aunt Evelyn's smile at the mention of Morris' name. Her aunt's offer to show Martha's paintings and letters became more and more alluring.

She explained to her parents that she wanted to visit Aunt Evelyn again.

"That's nice of you," her mother said. "She's pretty lonely and will probably appreciate your visit."

"She's an interesting lady, and I get to read Aunt Martha's letters."

"Aunt Martha's letters? That sounds fascinating. Be sure you give us a full report."

Her father chuckled. "You probably like the rum balls! My daughter, the lush."

"Oh, Dad!" Tivoli giggled. "Yeah, that's it. They are soooo good!"

After school, she walked the three miles to Hickory Manor. Gerard beamed when he opened the door, and she felt a welcoming freshness in the hallway, a sharp contrast to the air-dead, gloomy atmosphere of the parlor. When he escorted her into the room with the painted wall, her aunt walked toward her with a strong, sure stride, smiling broadly. She grasped Tivoli's hands. "I'm glad you took time out of your day to call on an old woman."

"I appreciate the invitation, and I like listening to your stories about the past," Tivoli told her, surprised at her own confidence. She placed her book bag on the couch beside her.

"It's good to see the young people using rucksacks. When I attended school, we carried all our books in one arm, which was bad for the posture."

"When was that, Aunt Evelyn?"

"I graduated from Clearwater High School back in 1938, a few years before the Second World War. Many boys from my class came home wounded, or didn't come home at all."

"Did that include Morris?"

Aunt Evelyn smiled – a sad smile, Tivoli thought. "Yes."

"What happened to him?"

Her aunt hesitated and let out a sigh. "He was killed somewhere in France."

The girl stood up and walked to the wall. Running her fingers over the painted trees and meadow, she felt cracks in the wood.

"Stand by me," Aunt Evelyn directed. "Then you can see the whole panorama at a glance. Martha actually created the scene from memory. In those days, reprints and postcards of paintings did not exist."

Tivoli scanned the grass, bushes, and trees, and to one side, a sandy beach with blue water beyond. On the opposite shore, loomed woods, under a gray-blue sky. In the left bottom corner, she saw the masses of purple flowers that had intrigued her on her last visit.

The woman touched the patch. "Lavender. Not in the original by Turner, nor were the two figures in the shadow of that tree. Martha added those, and the lavender has been touched up over and over again."

"Why?"

"Martha loved lavender and planted it all around the grounds, as you've no doubt noticed. And Cora did, too."

They drank tea, and her aunt inquired about various relatives. "Your grandma? My sister, Emma, how is she?"

"She's fine. Busy all the time. She has a whole lot of grandchildren, and she's always canning, crocheting, and giving us vegetables from her garden."

"Ah, yes, I can see her doing that. We're not at all alike, your grandmother and I. She comes to visit once a year, but I know she considers it a duty."

She rang the bell. "Gerard will escort us through the rest of the house so you can see Martha's paintings. Then, if you're interested, I'll take out her box of letters."

Unframed canvases hung throughout the house, but Tivoli was mostly intrigued by the mysterious rooms themselves. All had expansive windows, some with beveled glass. The late autumn sun cast rainbow hues into one large sitting area, and stained glass in bedrooms added warmth and color. Several windows were broken and cracked, yet shone with cleanliness.

"This house is impossible to heat," Aunt Evelyn said. "The walls leak air, so it's always drafty. We keep my sitting room, bedroom and kitchen in repair. That is all we can afford."

The furniture fascinated Tivoli. She did not know much about period styles, but she recognized an entirely different atmosphere in each room. She ran her hand over the curved back of a dining room chair. "Feels so smooth. It's beautiful!"

"Gerard's been collecting furniture for years."

As if waiting for a cue, Gerard stepped forward. "I'm glad you're interested, Miss. I do not get much chance to show off my treasures. The chairs in this room are all Windsor, from the time of the American Revolution. They're still being built in Maine today, but these are originals."

As they walked, their steps echoed in tall rooms with hardwood floors. In others, richly-woven Persian carpets muffled the sound.

Gerard pointed out the Victorian furniture in a bedroom. American Arts and Crafts pieces from the early 1900's stood in a closed-in porch, and an English Chippendale chest from the 16th century graced another bedroom. "There's so much here, Miss. You're welcome to come back, and I'll explain it all to you, one room at a time."

Tivoli promised herself that she would take him up on his offer. Where did all this priceless furniture come from? Her father said Evelyn had enough inheritance to take care of her daily needs, but not enough to fix up the house, let alone, acquire all this furniture. Who *was* this Gerard, really?

Returning to Aunt Evelyn's sitting room, the woman opened an ornate wooden chest and pulled out several bundles of yellowed letters tied together with faded purple ribbons.

"Martha's letters to William Turner. They are too fragile to travel, but Gerard will fix you a warm corner in the kitchen, so you can come and read them any time you want."

"My father said that Martha only met William one time. Why did she write all these letters? Did she send them and make copies, or were they never sent? Did he answer her?"

"Turner was a spoiled, arrogant man. I think she loved the paintings, conjured up Turner in her own mind, and fell in love with an image she herself created. That's quite possible, you know."

Tivoli noticed that her aunt had not directly answered her question.

Aunt Evelyn took a letter out of a packet and gave it to Tivoli. "This was her first letter. You can read it to yourself, if you want."

Tivoli unfolded the delicate paper. The dim glow of the lamp beside the couch gave her enough light to read the beautiful, ornate script from the hand of her distant ancestor.

"Darling William, how happy I am to finally have you here, close to me, where I can visit you any time! When I see you sitting at the edge of the lavender field and watch yet another beautiful seascape come alive on your easel, my heart fills with pride to know that you are finally mine. Next time I come, I know of a lovely tea garden not far away, where we could spend a leisurely afternoon. That is, if you have time, and if you are not in the middle of a project you cannot leave. How many hours it must have taken to paint that three-masted schooner! I never want to take you away from that which you most love. You have so much to give to the world!"

Tivoli glanced toward the painting and felt gooseflesh creeping on her arms. Beyond the field of lavender lay an inlet large enough to hold a sailing vessel, like the tall ships she had seen in history books. The tea garden could be hidden around a corner, beyond the scene. In fact, she had seen a large inn, ringed with white-clothed tables and wooden chairs in one of Martha's paintings.

Tivoli did not want to walk home in the dank, cold air that threatened snow, so she and ran to catch a bus and breathed a sigh of relief as the well-lit vehicle stopped. She climbed in, snuggled up against a window, and thought about the last few hours.

Did she really want to go back? She liked Gerard and Aunt Evelyn, but the wall scared her. Martha's words – what did she mean, *You are finally mine*. Who *was* this lady? Perhaps if she read the rest of the letters, she'd find out.

Christmas was just a few weeks away, and choir rehearsals kept Tivoli busy three nights a week. Her parents would have the family over this year, so her mother needed her to help decorate the house and bake cookies. There was no time for a visit to Hickory Manor.

By late January, Tivoli could contain her curiosity no longer. She longed to have tea with Aunt Evelyn, cuddle up in Gerard's breakfast nook in the kitchen, and read Martha's letters. The wall painting was etched in her mind and showed up when she dozed off to sleep, when she daydreamed at school, when she walked to the grocery store.

She dialed Gerard's number. He answered after one ring, friendly as always, and told her she was welcome to come and stay as long as she liked.

The following Wednesday, as soon as school was out, she rushed to Hickory Manor. After stopping in the sitting room to greet her aunt, she retreated to the cozy kitchen. A Franklin stove warmed the corner where she opened the first packet of letters. The next few hours flew by, leaving her enchanted, mystified, and more curious than ever.

The letters, written in ornate penmanship, made her wonder who Martha really was. Martha praised him for his landscapes, seascapes, and moody mountain paintings with ominous skies, people picnicking deep in the woods, and often, she mentioned the mirage-like mood he could bring to his paintings. Had she been a bright, pretty woman, very much in love with a man who was also deeply in love with her? Had she been all over the world with him, assisted him with his paintings, and, even carried on a romance?

Or had her great, great, great, great Aunt Martha been totally insane?

She asked Aunt Evelyn for books about William Turner and learned that Turner, born in 1775, had been twelve years older than Martha, had visited America only briefly, and had painted until well into the 1840's. Yet, the names of the paintings that were in Martha's letters made them seem as though they had all been created within a few years, while they were both young.

During the next weeks, Tivoli tried to put the pieces of the puzzle together. With the help of her great aunt, she learned that Hickory Manor had been built in 1820, and that Martha had inherited it ten years later, when she was no longer a young woman. Yet, the letters did not start until after she moved into the house, because the first was dated 1835.

Besides the books that Aunt Evelyn loaned her, she looked up Turner on the Internet and did a report on him for school.

Turner, the artist, had been an eccentric man with a quick temper. Although he never married, he lived with the widow of a friend for many years, and they had two children. Of other affairs, clandestine or public, she could find no evidence.

From her great aunt, she learned little more. No, Martha had certainly not been delusional. William Turner had very much been part of her life. But how was this possible?

Tivoli spent several afternoons over the next months reading Aunt Martha's letters. How could the ancestral aunt have lived a fantastic life, much of it in England, when she had visited there only briefly when she was young? It made no sense. Her considerable art talent was reflected in the letters. She made copious sketches of people in the margins, but also of "Papa," "Mama," and various other uncles, aunts, cousins, brothers, and sisters.

"Did Aunt Martha ever sell any of her paintings?" Tivoli asked Aunt Evelyn.

"Artistic talent was not valued or encouraged in women of that time, so she would not have had the chance to sell anything."

One day, as she was reading, Tivoli bolted upright and stared at a page in a letter. A sketch leaped out from the paper entitled, simply, "Gerard." The image was so clearly a likeness of Aunt Evelyn's servant, that she went in search of the elderly man. She found him in the back garden, dead-heading spent daffodils.

"Gerard!"

He looked up. "Yes, Miss?"

"I found a picture of somebody that looks just like you." She handed the sketch to him.

He looked at it thoughtfully. "What do you think, miss?"

"Maybe your father, or your grandfather. I don't know. But you look exactly like that, even the age."

Gerard's smile revealed nothing. "And you find this interesting, Miss Tivoli."

"Of course." But she sensed she should not pursue the mystery.

The days were longer now, so Tivoli walked home, mulling over the newest clues. The date on Martha's letter with the sketch was 1841. That was the year, apparently, that this servant arrived. Who was the person in the picture, and how could he have looked so much like Gerard?

She asked her father about Gerard.

"I've seen him all my life. So has everybody else in the village. Even when I was a boy, he looked exactly as he does now, or maybe that was his father. Nobody knows. People have tried to find out, but if anyone asks him directly, even to this day, he'll smile and talk about the weather or praise the quality of the tomatoes in the store.

"That sounds just like the Gerard I know, but how could that be?"

"Strange, isn't it? In my youth, I remember sneaking up to the house with a gang of junior high friends, fearful of encountering Aunt Evelyn, but hoping to find Gerard. He came to the back porch, smiled and waved, and went back inside.

"One time, before you were born, a photographer from a Memphis paper came to take pictures of the house, and some of us boys followed him. Gerard appeared at the back door. We all knew that the man hoped to be invited in, but Gerard just smiled his sunny smile. When he asked about his ancestors, he commented on the chestnut trees, which were in full bloom. He got absolutely nowhere with his questions."

Tivoli told her parents of her conversations with her aunt, of the house with many rooms and fine furniture, and about Aunt Martha's letters.

"You've given us details about the vague rumors we have heard for years, about the furniture and about the letters," her father said. "Your grandmother has known about some of this for a long time, but has never been particularly interested in *Evelyn's Fairy Land*, as she calls it. Has your aunt told you anything about the painting?"

"It was painted by Martha, from her memory of Turner's, *The West Country*, but she added figures and a field of lavender on one side."

"Ah, the lavender," her father mused. "Aunt Evelyn is obsessed with lavender. I wonder why it was so important for Martha to add it if it was not in the original?"

On her next visit, she touched the patch of lavender in the painting. And then she noticed something else – narrow rectangular slats that fitted over each other in a semi-circle, like a fan.

Her aunt got up and stood behind her. She pulled her necklace of keys from under her blouse and singled out a tiny gold object.

"It's time, Tivoli," she said.

"Time for what, Aunt Evelyn?"

"Time for you to learn the secret of the painting." She lifted the chain over her head and handed it to Tivoli. "The shaft of this key is very tiny, but if you look carefully, you'll see a hole in the center of top-most slat."

Tivoli found the hole, and, with trembling hands, she managed to fit the key into the miniscule lock. The slats slid over each other, opening up a half circle about three feet tall. A fresh breeze wafted from the opening. Beyond, she could see the vivid bluish-purple of lavender flower spikes waving in the breeze.

She gulped a quick breath. "Aunt Evelyn! What just happened? What *is* that?"

The woman's eyes shone with excitement. She put her hands on Tivoli's shoulders and guided her gently toward the opening. "That, my dear girl, is the window to a world of wonder – richer than Aladdin's cave, or The Secret Garden, or maybe even the Garden of Eden. We'll enter together!"

"But Aunt!"

"Oh, it's perfectly safe. Just stay with me. I promise you, you'll be home in time for dinner."

Full of apprehension and wonder, Tivoli stepped through the portal into the magical world that would change her life.

CHAPTER FOUR

A gentle breeze greeted Tivoli as she stood in a huge field of lavender, but she felt her heart race as she breathed in its fragrance. Where was she? How could this place be possible? Feeling dizzy, she grasped her aunt's arm and breathed deeply.

"Let's rest for a moment, child." Aunt Evelyn steered her to a flat rock, and Tivoli sat as her legs buckled under her. Her aunt's voice was soothing. "It will take you a bit of time to get used to this, but it's quite safe, really."

Tivoli turned to look at the wall. "How do we get out?" she asked, her voice shaky.

"Don't worry, dear. The way out is even easier than entering. We won't stay long, but I want you to look around, and when you feel up to it, we'll take a short walk."

The warmth of a gentle sun bathed Tivoli with its radiance. She allowed Aunt Evelyn to lead her on a dirt path that wove through the bushes to a meadow, and the scene before them resembled the painting. Tivoli guessed that, if they walked on, they would reach the inlet and the woods beyond. Though the wall painting was faded and dingy, the world it hid was brilliant with color.

Aunt Evelyn walked beside her, her body straight and tall, and she inhaled deeply. "What do you think of my world, Tivoli, dear?"

The girl glanced at her great aunt. The elderly face glowed with liveliness. Her eyes sparkled, and her step was so sprightly that Tivoli had to change her own pace to keep up. "It's, it's, I don't know what to say. It's beautiful, but I'm a bit scared. It's so big. There's nothing like this in Clearwater. So where are we? Does this place even exist?"

"Oh, it exists, all right, and you've only seen a small portion of it. In a few minutes, we'll walk along the shore."

Tivoli spied an expanse of water in the distance, and soon, they stepped onto a sparkling beige beach, dotted with sand dollars and shells. Tivoli picked up a conch and held it to her ear, as an ocean roared into her senses. Clutching the shell in her hand, she walked with her aunt back to the meadow, and they meandered through a herd of grazing sheep. A curly-bearded shepherd tipped his hat.

"Morning, ladies. How are you today, Miss Evelyn?"

"I am well, thank you, Jacob. I'd like you to meet my niece, Tivoli."

He extended his hand to the girl, and she felt his warm, firm grip. A yellow dog, long-haired with curly feathered paws, bounded toward them, and Tivoli held out her palm for him to sniff. He proffered his head for a good scratch.

Jacob laughed. "I see Goldie likes you, Tivoli. She's very choosy, so consider it a compliment!"

As they continued their walk, Tivoli marveled at the transformation in her aunt. The woman's vigor belied her years.

"We'll go back now, my girl. This is quite enough for one day. The next time you come, I will show you the village."

"The village? There's no village in the painting."

"The painting only scratches the surface. You have no idea yet what lies in store for you! This was merely a prelude."

They wandered back through the lavender to the wall. Aunt Evelyn touched the fan where they had entered, and they exited into the sitting room.

Tivoli sighed with relief, but noticed that her hand no longer held the shell. She must have dropped it coming through. After a quick goodbye, she left the manor and ran home, grateful to be in familiar surroundings.

The following week, she was haunted by indecision. Would she go back? Her curiosity took over and some of her apprehension waned. She called Gerard and asked if she could come just to talk to him.

"Drop by tomorrow after school, and I'll make tea for us in the kitchen."

As usual, the kitchen felt homey, and she relaxed in the presence of Gerard. He picked up a steaming pot of tea and poured them each a cup.

She lifted the cover. "Why is it so brown inside?"

"It's my favorite, and it has been seasoned by years of use. Your aunt insists on clean and scrubbed tea pots, but I think tea tastes better with the patina of all the Darjeerlings, Red Rose, Chinese, and spice teas that have ever graced the pot."

Tivoli asked, "Do you know the secret of the painting?"

Gerard slid a plate of peanut butter cookies toward her across the table. "Somewhat. Whenever I enter the sitting room and Miss O'Leary isn't there, I know she's visiting her special world."

Tivoli picked up a cookie and broke it in half. "Has Aunt Evelyn share it with many people?"

"Not at all. Since she's moved into Hickory Manor, you are the first person in the family who has ever gone through to the other side. That means that she has extraordinary trust in you, and I know she enjoys your visits. You brighten her life."

"But her life behind the painting seems plenty bright. I saw how she was when we were there – happy, with lots of energy."

"She needs happiness on this side, too," Gerard said. "She never gets out of her quarters, and her life is pretty dismal here."

Gerard picked up a few crumbs with a napkin. Tivoli smiled. It was part of his character, she decided – almost too tidy. "Why doesn't she ever leave? She could go into town and shop."

"I think she feels that people will stare at her and whisper behind her back. But mostly, she is afraid to leave the house. She has to be here every day."

"Why?"

Gerard looked out through the window with a dreamy expression on his face. "She'll need to explain."

Tivoli asked Gerard if she could see the furniture again, and he took her to several rooms she had not seen on her last excursion. They entered a large sitting area with a collection of stained-glass lamps.

"I've heard about Tiffany lamps at school. Are any of these Tiffany?"

Gerard smiled, sweeping his arm around the room. "All of them!"

"All? But aren't they terribly expensive?"

"Most, yes. I have several books that show many more through the ages, as well as books about different furniture periods. You are welcome to come any time and browse through them."

Tivoli told her parents about the furniture collection, because she felt it was the only way she could explain her desire to go to Hickory Manor as often as possible. With their blessing, she spent the following Saturday curled up in Gerard's breakfast nook. She spread the volumes out in front of her on the table.

"I suggest you begin with one period or style," Gerard advised her.

But her fascination with the world behind the painting haunted Tivoli, even in her dreams. How could a painting open up and place her in a space that didn't exist? How did this ever get started? Did Martha's fantasy about William Turner have something to do with this virtual world?

She had to find out more. The following week, she called Gerard and asked for another visit with Aunt Evelyn. Tivoli hurried from school to have tea, a ritual the girl looked forward to, as much as she wanted to step through the wall again.

"I knew you would return," her aunt said, smiling. "But I figured that you needed to think about your experience here last time. You must have questions about the world beyond the painting."

"Yes, I do, Aunt Evelyn. Did Martha know about it? She kept writing about this William as though she was there, with him."

"You're catching on. Cora and I have always called this simply, Martha's World."

She took out her keys and found the tiny one, while walking toward the patch of lavender. Placing the key in its slot, the elderly woman waited until it opened and they walked through. The wall closed behind them, and they were again in the pristine, yet mysterious environment that had haunted the girl for the past week.

Aunt Evelyn increased her pace. "Let's walk to the village." They turned right this time, past the wall, and around a corner that Tivoli had never seen in the painting. At once, she saw a group of half-timbered houses with thatched roofs that reminded her of pictures of English cottages, but also chalets she had seen in photographs of Switzerland. Behind, loomed snow-capped mountains.

"Wow! Aunt Evelyn! Does it ever snow here?"

"Only if I want it to."

"What would so much snow do to the thatch, if it stayed on a long time?"

"It would not deteriorate, if that's what you mean."

"Do people ski here?"

"I never thought about it, but you can, if you want to."

They passed casually-dressed people, some with walking sticks and heavy hiking shoes, old men in Lederhosen, and young men in U.S. military uniforms from another time, complete with medals and insignia. Tivoli stared at women in jumpers with short-sleeved blouses, open-toed shoes, and long page-boy hairdos, or with knots of curls pinned above their foreheads. Some wore brown and white shoes, with anklets.

Aunt Evelyn followed her gaze. "Saddle shoes and bobby socks. And you're not supposed to clean the shoes. At least, that was the custom at that time."

They walked further, while Tivoli peered into a shop windows and scanned crowds of shoppers.

They reached an outdoor café. "Why not have a seat, Tivoli?" Aunt Evelyn said. "There's plenty here to look at. I'll be back shortly." She strolled away, around the corner.

Tivoli sat down and felt a moment of panic, but forced herself to relax as she basked in the warm sunshine bathing her face. The parade of people grew. Several couples walked past her: women dressed in skirts with fitted jackets, linking arms with trim, young men in white Naval officer uniforms from another time, complete with shoulder epaulettes. A waiter came toward her, but she waved him away. She had no money. Or would she even need money here?

As the minutes passed, she grew frightened. When was Aunt Evelyn coming back, if ever? Could she get out by herself? What was she doing here, anyway?

"Tivoli!"

Startled to hear a lilting voice behind her, she stood up and turned to watch the approach of a tall young woman, in her early twenties. The radiant face was framed by auburn hair that hung loosely and curled under. She wore a white blouse and an ankle-length skirt.

"Don't you recognize your old Aunt Evelyn?" The gray-blue eyes sparkled with merriment.

Frightened, Tivoli stepped back and stared.

"It's all right, dear. Soon I'll change again, and we will go back to the *real* world."

"But Aunt, how could you do that?"

"You'll be able to, as well. You told me how your teacher became Abraham Lincoln. People take on different parts in plays all the time."

"In a play, you can make a young person look old with makeup and padding, but it's pretty hard to make an old person look young!"

Smiling, the woman flipped back her hair with a hand. "That's true, unless, of course, you can change the time. We're in 1943 now. Would you like something to drink? Verner's Ginger Ale is my favorite." She gestured to the waiter, and he came forward, smiling.

"Miss O'Leary, I'm honored to serve you! I see you've brought a young friend."

"Yes, this is Miss Hansen."

Tivoli noticed that her aunt did not call her a great-niece.

"We would each like a ginger ale, please. And put it on my tab."

After he left, Tivoli asked, "Tab, Aunt Evelyn? Do you pay?"

Her aunt laughed. "Oh, no, that's just a pretended formality. And you can call me Evelyn here, or just Evvy."

Tivoli stared at the woman, charmed by her beauty and vivaciousness. Friendly people passed by and noticed them. "Good to see you, Evelyn!"

"Evvy! You're a sight for sore eyes!"

"How is the gorgeous Miss O'Leary today?"

Several soldiers passed by. "Hubba hubba," they called.

Tivoli giggled. "'Hubba hubba?' What language is that?"

Evelyn waved to the young men. "That is very much early 40's American. And it's meant for pretty girls, like you, dear Tivoli."

"And you, Evvy!"

Two men, dressed in khaki slacks, open-collared shirts and vests, strolled up. "Hello, ladies," said the taller of the two, smiling at Evelyn. "Join us at Grady's? There's a great little band today, and they know all the Jitterbug tunes!"

Surprised at their charm and boldness, Tivoli watched her transformed aunt and was even more astounded. The now-young woman smiled with flirtatious coyness. "Oh, we'd love to, but my friend is too young to go inside, and besides, we're waiting for someone."

They left with the same cheerfulness as when they had arrived, and Tivoli, puzzled by this environment that seemed eerily normal, asked, "We're waiting for someone?"

"Yes, he'll be along soon."

Tivoli glanced about. More people walked by, nodding to them or speaking brief greetings. "Afternoon, Evvy."

Suddenly, Evelyn got up, and, with a bounce in her step, walked toward a tall man in a white Navy uniform. He took off his hat and held it in one hand, as he opened his arms. They kissed briefly, and Evvy steered him back to the table.

"Darling, I want you to meet a friend of mine. And, Tivoli, *this* is Morris."

CHAPTER FIVE

That night, Tivoli lay awake, haunted by the image of the handsome couple: her aunt and the mysterious Morris. Their closeness, their obvious passion for each other, the village, the friendly people, the cloudless sky and warm sun, were all so perfect that it scared her, but she knew she wanted to go back. She would not share this with anyone – not her parents, not even her cousins. Aunt Evelyn knew that, she was sure, or she would never have revealed Martha's World to her, and certainly not Morris.

But Morris? Aunt Evelyn herself had told Tivoli that he had died during the war. Grandma had said that Morris and Evelyn had broken their engagement a year before he went overseas. She wondered about the village. Where did it come from? Where was the space for all of this? She knew that on the other side of the mural lay Aunt Evelyn's bedroom. But most intriguing was the revelation about

Aunt Evelyn herself. Her aunt could be the stunningly beautiful Evvy any time she chose.

The next morning, Tivoli leaned sleepily on one elbow as she dumped cereal and splashed milk into a bowl.

Her mother sat down and reached across the kitchen table. Cupping Tivoli's chin in her hand, she lifted up her daughter's face. "Are you all right? I heard you get up several times during the night."

"Yeah, I'm fine, Mom. Just couldn't sleep very well."

"How are things at Hickory Manor? You were there again yesterday, weren't you?"

Tivoli evaded her mother's probing eyes. If her mother guessed she held something back, she might not let her return to Aunt Evelyn and Gerard.

She feigned enthusiasm. "Gerard showed me a new room full of Shaker furniture yesterday, and he has books about Shaker crafts. He told me all about Sabbath Lake in Maine, where a few remaining Shakers still live."

"Did you see Aunt Evelyn?"

"Oh, yes. We always have tea when I arrive. It's our ritual."

Her mother drew a deep breath. "Your English teacher called yesterday to say that you haven't been turning in your homework, and that you seem to be daydreaming instead of paying attention in class."

"I'm tired because of band practice after school."

"Well, for the next two weeks, I want you to stay away from Hickory Manor. You need to catch up on your homework and get more rest."

Tivoli slumped down in her chair. She knew it was useless to argue, and decided not to push her luck.

On Saturday, her cousin, Johanna Jackson, called about her pending visit to Aunt Evelyn. Tivoli told her that their great-aunt was nice enough, but very formal, that the house was spooky, and that Gerard would help the girl feel at ease. On the day that Johanna was to visit Hickory Manor, Tivoli felt apprehensive. What if Aunt Evelyn confided in her cousin, too? What if she introduced her to Martha's World? But Gerard had said that Tivoli had been the only person to ever be invited into that secret place.

Tivoli caught up with homework in all her classes and surprised her mother by vacuuming all the carpets and polishing the furniture. In the library, she checked out books about Shakers, found articles on the web, and started a project for her history class. Thoughts about Martha's World roiled through her mind, but she forced them away.

At the end of the two weeks, she called Gerard and asked if she could spend Saturday at the Manor.

Blossoming cherry trees flanked the house and the meandering driveway, and the pale pink flowers softened the foreboding appearance of the entrance. When Gerard opened the door, Tivoli hugged him.

He smiled. "Welcome, dear girl. Your aunt awaits you."

Tivoli greeted her aunt and sat down on the couch. Gerard brought coffee for Aunt Evelyn and hot chocolate for Tivoli.

Tivoli leaned forward. "Aunt Evelyn, I've got so many questions!"

The elderly woman smiled. "Were you surprised to see your transformed aunt?"

"Yes, and Morris, especially. I thought you said he was killed during that Nazi war."

"That's World War II, my dear. Yes, he was killed, but I brought him back alive behind the wall."

"*Really* alive? Like his bones are not lying around, rotting?"

Her great aunt laughed. "Oh, his remains are buried, all right, but that's not the real Morris. Neither is the one you saw, I suppose, but he's real enough to me."

"How did he get there? And that village? And those people? None of that is in the painting."

Evelyn poured another cup of cocoa for Tivoli. "That's the magic of Martha's World, with additions from Cora. Cora created the village, and I kept it. Only the people are different: 1940s characters who love Frank Sinatra and listen to Fibber McGee and Molly. They watch *Gone with the Wind*, swoon over Clark Gable, and dance the Jitterbug. Soldiers put posters in their lockers of Betty Grable, showing off her famous legs."

"I've heard of some of those stars, and my parents and I watched a DVD of *Gone with the Wind* when I was studying the Civil War at school. Awesome story!"

"I'm glad to hear how much your parents support your education," said Aunt Evelyn. "And I hope you are keeping up with your school work. I realize that learning about Martha's World may be a distraction, but what you will learn there will show you a different way to view history and geography."

"What do you mean, Aunt Evelyn?"

"Behind that wall, I can travel, and so can you, anywhere in the world. All I have to do is create with my mind, and it will take shape. The next time I visit I can change it, if I want to, like re-touching an oil painting, but with my brain. If I make a mistake or do not like what I have created, I can start over."

Tivoli sipped her cocoa. "What I saw, then, is what you or Cora or Martha created. It is your imaginations that I visited, not my own."

"That is correct, but you can do it, too. You can add or take out anything you wish in that world and go anywhere, but you have to be careful. You must always be able to find the wall, because that's the only normal way you can get out."

"There's another?"

"One time, using information from *National Geographic* and library books about Australia, I created my own out-back area, complete with kangaroos, Aborigines, and Ayers Rock. After spending an afternoon by the Rock, I wanted to return, but became disoriented. I was terrified, because Cora had warned me that I might never return to the real world if I got lost, so I walked faster, then ran. The scenery became blurred and jumbled, and ground vines grabbed my legs until I stumbled and fell. The plants twined around my body, until I was suffocating."

"That sounds horrible. What happened next?"

"That is all I remember, until I awoke on the floor in my bedroom, on the other side of the mural. After that, I stayed in familiar territory for a few weeks before I ventured out again. I feared that next time I wouldn't come back at all. So you must know where the wall is, at all times."

Tivoli shivered and stared at the painting. "How can you get lost in a space that doesn't even exist?"

"I know it doesn't make sense, to the rational mind."

Tivoli picked up a *National Geographic* that lay on the table beside her. "Aunt Evelyn, you mean, I can go to Australia behind the mural?"

"Well, yes, at least the Australia that I have created in my mind, aided by photographs in books and magazines. I've never been to any of those places."

"Have you ever traveled, Aunt Evelyn?"

"Some. In 1938, when I was eighteen and before I moved into the house, I went with my parents to England for a three-week vacation. We traveled by subway all over London, then by motorcar to Stonehenge, and we visited relatives in a coal-mining town in Wales. The people were good to us, but they were so poor.

"I did not want that in my world, so I've been able to create happy, beautiful places. From the wall, you can visit the French Riviera, Mexico, Hawaii, a small village in Brazil, an island off the coast of Greece, a town at the foot of Mount Kilimanjaro. I've designed them all. You can change them, put in people you love, and create activities. I think you mentioned skiing, Tivoli."

"What about horseback riding?"

"If you wish. You can fashion a horse to your liking and ride him until you're saddle-sore! All the exercise I need, I get in there as a young woman, walking, paddling a canoe, and..."

"And what, Aunt Evelyn?"

"Oh, never mind."

The woman looked down, but Tivoli saw a faint smile.

Morris.

"How often do you go in there? Into Martha's World, I mean?"

"I enter every day. Sometimes I enter in the morning, sometimes not until late afternoon. But if I do not go in each day, then when I visit again, the original scene, which is the replica of the painting, has begun to fade somewhat. I have to repair it with my mind before I dare venture beyond the scene itself, into my own creations."

"Repair? What do you mean? I don't understand."

"It's hard to explain, but you have a lot to learn, and I will teach you.

"Once, when I was ill for a few days, I opened the lavender gate each day, but had no energy to go inside. When I was well enough again, the scene had become quite unstable. Even the lavender in the foreground had faded, and I felt myself sinking into the ground with each step. I needed quite a while that time to bring it back to its original state. Martha believed if she stayed away for ten days, Martha's World would be completely gone. Cora thought so, too. None of us has ever tested that theory."

Tivoli sat on the edge of the couch, staring at the lavender patch as she listened to her aunt. "You mean you can't leave? Can't even go on vacation?"

"No. That is the trade-off, but I take more beautiful and exotic vacations than anyone I know, anytime, and for free! Why would I want to go anywhere else?"

Tivoli felt a wave of apprehension, but she brushed it away. "How about Gerard? Can't he maintain it for you?"

"No, he cannot."

"Why not, Aunt Evelyn?"

Her aunt did not answer the question, but walked over and retrieved the wooden box that had contained Martha's letters. "Besides the letters, Martha also kept a diary. If you like, you can read that as well, when you spend time in Gerard's kitchen."

"How did it ever get started, this door and the world beyond?"

"That is the great mystery, but you'll find some clues in the diary, where she described her progress as she painted the wall. She told of her yearning to enter the painting. She even hired an engineer to design the sliding panels." Aunt Evelyn rose and walked to the painting, touching the lavender slats. "Anyone can touch it, but without the key, nothing will happen, so she asked the man to make a lock and a key."

"He must have thought she was out of her mind!"

"Probably, but he did what she asked, and with the key, Martha could finally open it, but to a solid wall behind. That was a great disappointment, of course, but she kept on imagining exactly the way she wanted it to work, and one day, when she opened the latch with the key, she felt a breath of spring air and saw sun-lit lavender beyond the wall. She was afraid, but stepped through."

Tivoli peered through the portal and breathed deeply.. "That's right, Aunt Evelyn. I can feel the breeze, and it smells like outside, after a rainstorm." She stepped into the arch of lavender, and her aunt followed.

"How do you create a scene?"

"Come! I'll show you. You can try something simple first."

As before, the sky was the brilliant blue of a radiant summer day.

"Your wish, my dear?" her aunt asked.

"A horse that I can ride all over these meadows, and into the town, and by the seashore!"

"That's a bit advanced for a first try, but I'll create one so I can show you the process. First, I fix my eyes on where I want the horse to appear: on that grass in the distance, close to the water would be a good place."

Aunt Evelyn's eyes glazed over. Except for the deep breaths that moved her chest, the woman stood very still. Tivoli followed her gaze toward the distant meadow and saw an amorphous blob at first, but then it became clearer, more pronounced, until a jet-black stallion pranced in the distant meadow.

Tivoli clapped and jumped up and down. "Awesome, Aunt Evelyn! That's awesome!"

"Yes, a beauty, if I say so myself. I'll call him Stallion. Now it's your turn. First, close your eyes and take some deep breaths. With enough practice, the technique will become effortless, but at first, you need to compose yourself. We're going to sit here on this rock for a few minutes until you feel very calm."

As she sat, the sun bathing her face, Tivoli relaxed, breathing deeply. She squinted and saw the stallion in the sunlight.

Aunt Evelyn asked, "Have you seen pictures that seem to make no sense at first, but when you stare at them in a certain way, you see three-dimensional figures appear?"

"My father has a book of those. It has something to do with how details are spaced across the picture."

"Somewhat like that, yes. As you relax your eyes, you create an extra image in the center. Put your forefingers together in front of your eyes, like this." Evelyn held her hands ten inches in front of her eyes. "What do you see?"

Tivoli imitated. "Two fingers with a funny little sausage finger in between!"

"That is what you do with your eyes. Look at a patch of grass and then see, in your mind, the horse you want. Next thing you know, you'll create what you see, right onto the meadow!"

Tivoli focused, then un-focused her eyes. She saw a roan mare in her mind and tried to place it on the patch, but nothing happened.

"You're trying too hard. Relax. See it again. Then see the grass. Then the horse. Then place them together."

This time, she made out a blotch of light brown, but without much form. "I think something's happening, Aunt Evelyn!"

"Yes, I see it, too. Close your eyes again, then open them and stay relaxed."

The form became clearer, and finally, a mare sprang into shape, prancing in profile.

"There she is! I did it!"

"Good work! Now, bring her closer. Just keep watching her and will her to come to us."

The horse turned and moved toward them. She wobbled as if still learning how to walk, but then became more sure of her stride and trotted, nickering, her mane blowing in the wind.

Evelyn reached down to pluck a sprig of lavender and held it out. The horse sniffed, then grasped it with gentle lips and ate hungrily.

Tivoli stroked the face and nose. The skin felt warm and she lay her head against the mare's neck, breathing in the familiar equine odor.

"I've only been on a horse once before. I'd like to get on her back, but she has no saddle, and I don't even know if I can get on."

"You won't need a saddle. You can ride her bareback. Since she's your horse, she'll do whatever you like."

Her aunt helped her mount the mare's back. "Just hang on to her mane. You can steer her that way." The horse trotted slowly, keeping pace with Aunt Evelyn.

"Let's round the corner here, and we'll create a paddock for her and for Stallion."

A few minutes later, the scene was set. Evelyn encouraged Tivoli to add fence posts and rails. With a backdrop of hills and woods, the enclosure was now complete with a feeding trough, a small pond, and soft green grass. They led the horses into the enclosure.

"We'd better go back now," Aunt Evelyn said. "I need to take my medicine."

"Can I stay for a while by myself?"

Aunt Evelyn took both of Tivoli's hands into her own and gazed into her eyes. "I'll let you stay, but come back soon. Don't go beyond that tree. If you're not back in fifteen minutes, I'll worry about you, since you are so new to all of this. Above all, always remember how to get back to the wall." She gave Tivoli's hands a squeeze. "You will not need the key. Just touch the right spot on the latch, and it will open for you. Good luck, and be careful!"

Aunt Evelyn hugged her and walked away.

Tivoli stood alone in a world her aunt had created, with some of her own additions. Many times in her mind, she had built imaginary scenes and been a major player. But here she was, in her own virtual reality.

She walked the mare back out and to a small pond. The animal drank with big slurps, and Tivoli leaned her head against the warm flank. *My horse. My very own horse, and I created her. I wonder what name she'd like?*

"Wanda?" she said.

The horse did not react, but kept on drinking.

"Of course not! Wanda was a fish, in some old movie. How about Beauty? No, that's far too common. But you are beautiful. Natasha?"

The horse turned and looked at her.

"That's a Russian name. You like it? Natasha." The mare nudged her with her nose.

"Well, Natasha, would you like to go for a walk? Aunt Evelyn doesn't want us to go far, so we'll just go to the water."

She mounted and dug her legs into the horse's flank. She tugged the mane to the right, and the horse responded by turning slightly. Natasha walked wherever Tivoli thought to go. Tivoli watched the familiar landscape from the painting pass by. When she saw new scenery, she felt a twinge of uneasiness. She glanced back toward the wall.

She steered the horse toward a stand of trees, and along a path. When she reached a clearing, the ocean came into view, its roar thundering in her ears. She led Natasha onto the firm beach sand.

Her fear vanished. "We'll go just a little ways. We'll be all right." Excited, she kicked Natasha into a trot. Evelyn must have created this scene. Or Cora. Or even Martha herself. Along the shore were more trees, a continuation of the forest.

"What do you think, Natasha? Could I clear the trees and build a little cabin?" She walked the horse closer to the patch of forest and singled out a large cedar.

"I'll pretend I'm a logger!" Tivoli focused and unfocused her gaze, until the top of the massive tree swayed from side to side. She heard a crack and watched as the cedar began to topple.

Suddenly gripped with fear, she thought, *What if it comes this way?* As the splintering trunk crackled with a loud chattering, the top of the tree suddenly darkened the sky and careened toward her.

"Run, Natasha!" Tivoli screamed. The horse obeyed, lunging with such force that Tivoli lost her balance and fell onto the soft sand. She scrambled to her knees and tried to stand up, but her feet skidded. She crawled, panting. A branch landed on her leg, new and supple, but strong enough to pin her down.

Tivoli cried out. Her leg hurt and she tried to pull away, but her tennis shoe was wedged firmly between a rock and the branch. She tugged her foot hard, and it came free, leaving the shoe behind.

Shaken, she hobbled toward Natasha, who waited while Tivoli balanced on her uninjured leg and hoisted herself to the mare's back. Her ankle throbbed, and she winced with pain.

She clutched Natasha's mane. "We'll follow the shore. That way, we can't get lost. Or can we?" The scene ahead of her blurred. The shoreline grew dim. "What if it changes and we can't go back the same way?" The panorama ahead shifted again, and her body tensed with panic.

"Get a grip," she said aloud. "Is my fear making all this happen? It was only after my panic that the scene had shifted. I'd been scared the tree was going to fall on me, and…"

Tivoli focused her mind on the lavender and as she rounded the bend, she saw the comforting, familiar bay, the flowers, and the wall in the distance. She wanted to leave Natasha in the meadow to graze, but knew that this would change the original scene, so she led the horse back to the paddock.

The walk back to the wall seemed endless, and her leg felt as though on fire. She picked up a stick on the path to use as a cane. She leaned heavily on it as she limped toward the wall, the sock of her shoeless foot caked with dirt. She wondered how she was going to explain the limp and the missing shoe. And how could she possibly walk home?

Needing to rest, Tivoli sat on a rock, rubbing her ankle. Maybe she could create a shoe! She looked at a patch of dirt, focusing and un-focusing until a left shoe appeared – scuffed and soiled, and the mirror image of her right one. But when she tried to put it on, her foot was too swollen, so she carried the shoe, finally reaching the wall.

The door was already open, and Aunt Evelyn, a worried look on her face, walked toward her.

"Lean on me, child. We'll have to ice that leg before you go home."

Evelyn helped the girl back toward the portal. Tivoli leaned the stick against the wall, then stepped through, clutching the shoe in her right fist. Once inside Aunt Evelyn's sitting room, she limped to the couch.

Her hand was empty.

CHAPTER SIX

Evelyn picked up her phone and spoke briefly to Gerard. He arrived with an Ace bandage and an ice pack. With deft, gentle hands, he wrapped Tivoli's ankle, and the cold eased the pain almost immediately.

Her great aunt moved to the couch and held the girl's hand. "What happened?"

Tivoli explained the ride along the shore and her encounter with the tree. "I didn't know I could get hurt in there!"

"Only if you're afraid. I guess you already discovered that. You can actually get rid of trees by just thinking them away. That's much safer, but I should have warned you. I thought you would come right back, and I didn't want to alarm you."

Tivoli glanced at her watch. "It's 7:00! I've got to get home, but I can't walk."

"Gerard will call your parents so they won't worry. And, as soon as your leg feels a little better, he'll drive you home."

"I lost my shoe and created another one, but it's gone, too."

"You can't take anything from Martha's World outside, and nothing you bring in can stay when you leave." Aunt Evelyn got up. "I'll be right back."

She walked toward the bedroom and returned with Tivoli's shoe. "It was lying on the other side of the wall near my bed. It looks a little mashed, but you can probably pull it back into shape."

"What'll I tell my parents about my ankle?"

"Tell them you tripped coming down the stairs."

Tivoli tugged at her shoe and frowned. "But Aunt Evelyn. That's not what happened."

"True, but it's best not to alarm your parents."

On her way home with Gerard in the station wagon, she pondered Aunt Evelyn's remark. Tivoli would have made up a story herself without the slightest twinge of guilt, but how could her proper Aunt even suggest such a thing?

School ended in mid-June, and that summer, Tivoli took every chance she could to go to Hickory Manor. Sometimes she talked to Gerard about furniture and visited her favorite rooms.

She roamed with Aunt Evelyn, who often became "Evvy" on their travels. It seldom took long to get anywhere. When they wanted to visit the pyramids near Cairo, Evvy parted a thicket of bushes and they were at Giza, staring at the Great Pyramid.

They were only minutes away from Red Square, the Great Wall of China, the Taj Mahal. Was it too perfect? At times, Tivoli wanted to feel that she traveled far away from home, and that it took time and effort to get somewhere

After returning from a trip to Iceland, Aunt Evelyn said, "Next time we enter Martha's World, I'll take you to an amphitheater for a concert."

"A concert, Aunt Evelyn, but how could this be?"

"It was the most challenging of my creations and took a long time."

As promised, on Tivoli's next visit, Aunt Evelyn led the way past the village to a grassy knoll. As they rounded a bend, they were high above a bowl-shaped theater with rocks and logs for seats and a large wooden stage in the center. Chairs faced an empty conductor's dais. Framing the stage, stood a row of tall poplar trees.

As they watched, people walked onto the stage carrying violins and bassoons, and rolling in a timpani section, a harp, and a grand piano. The audience wandered in and found seats.

When the tableau looked complete, Aunt Evelyn disappeared briefly. The oboe played an "A," the concert master rose, repeated the note on his violin, and the orchestra tuned their instruments.

Her aunt reappeared on stage, wearing a shimmering black floor-length dress with long sleeves. She had not become Evvy, but remained the vibrant, energetic octogenarian persona of Aunt Evelyn. She bowed, and the orchestra stood as they, and the audience, applauded.

In a clear,resonant voice, she announced, "For our first selection, we will play the slow movement from Edgar Elgar's *Enigma Variations*."

Aunt Evelyn turned to the players and, lifting a baton, directed the violins, the flutes, and the cellos into a dreamy melody that brought wistful tears to Tivoli's eyes. The music swelled, faded, and then swelled again slowly, majestically. The basses and the drums added depth and drama to the piece. It ended softly and seemed to drift out and over the valley.

Aunt Evelyn returned, and together, they walked back toward the wall.

"That was beautiful, but how?" Tivoli asked, in utter amazement. She stared at Aunt Evelyn, who looked drained and exhausted, yet exhilarated.

"It's difficult, but you can do it, too. I listen to a recording, a few phrases at a time – part of a melody, maybe only an instrument that I have memorized, and I teach it to one section, or to a solo instrument. If it sounds too thin, I listen some more, add to the flute section, strengthen the clarinets or the drums, and enhance the piece. A little more each time, more and more and more, until one day, I know in my heart that it's complete. One movement from one symphony can take me months."

They walked on, and Tivoli played with a rock on the dirt path, kicking it with one foot and then the other. "What are some of your other pieces, Aunt Evelyn?"

"I've specialized in British composers. I have created a few piano sonatas by John Field. The piano is a challenge, and I have to go back to work out each hand alone, then coordinate with the other. And I've done other Elgar variations and some Ralph Vaughn Williams music."

"In my band, we play *Pomp and Circumstance* by that Mr. Elgar," Tivoli said. "Have you done that?"

Evelyn took hold of Tivoli's hand as they walked on. "No, but we can study it together, and I can help you add it to the repertoire. That has wonderful drama."

"How about *Bolero*? I love *Bolero*!"

"Not English, of course, but no reason why you can't create it. I'm not sure you'd want to live with that piece of music for months, though. It may drive you crazy!"

"Aunt Evelyn, you looked wonderful on that stage, but why weren't you Evvy?"

"Evvy's lives in the '40's and loves the popular music of that time. She doesn't have the depth and appreciation of classical music that I've developed in maturity."

They were approaching the wall. Tivoli savored the last few minutes of the warm sun on her back before breaking through to the dreary, windy day in her own world.

But she knew she could come back any time on her own, by herself, so she could be with Natasha. In the weeks that followed, she often went in for short periods of time, content to walk the horse to a nearby stream and sit with her feet dangling in cool water. As the mare drank, Tivoli groomed the animal and talked to her.

Fall activities kept Tivoli from Hickory Manor until after the new year when she visited Aunt Evelyn and Gerard with a plate of home-made cookies.

"Thank you, child, it's good to see you," Aunt Evelyn said, sipping the tea Gerard had just poured. "I realize school becomes more involved these days, and homework is more complicated as you get older. But I hope you'll visit when you can."

Tivoli promised but had little chance until the school year was over. Meanwhile, she dreamed of scenes she would create when she could spend more time in Martha's World.

That summer she tried, and at first, she could not make anything happen; but with her aunt's help, she now had her own cabin with a loft, and, using her mind, she reproduced pieces of furniture from Gerard's collection.

One day, when she reached the cabin with Natasha, Tivoli decided to explore a path that led into a forest. She found switchbacks wide enough for the horse, and they climbed until they entered a clearing. A broad valley lay before her, with snow-capped mountains in the distance.

The path continued through a grassy meadow, thick with brilliant wildflowers and a stream. Tivoli let Natasha drink as she dismounted and cupped her hands to capture the clear, cold water. It tasted pure and sweet. She wondered, as she had a few other times, how she could take this water in her body back out through the wall, but somehow, that seemed possible. She recalled now that she had never felt the need to urinate while in Martha's World. Would Aunt Evelyn know? Then remembered that she often rushed to the bathroom near the kitchen, after she left the mural.

She resumed her journey. Around a hill, she saw a large building in the distance. Curious, she patted Natasha's head and kicked the mare's sides. The horse cantered toward the low, gray structure. A huge veranda encircled the building, and soon Tivoli could make out the movement of people.

She slowed the horse and guided her to a stand of trees, then jumped off and ordered Natasha to wait. Tivoli walked cautiously, aware that some of the figures on the expansive porch sat in wooden wheel chairs. Others hobbled on wooden crutches, while many walked with canes.

As she approached, they noticed her. "Help me, miss! Please help! It's hot out here. I need water," someone cried.

Tivoli's heart raced. She stood still and waited. The same man repeated his plea, over and over in a sing-song mantra. No one moved out of place more than a few yards. The people on crutches performed their wobbly motions again and again.

Just expect them all to be harmless, Tivoli told herself, remembering what her mind could do if she gave in to fear. Once on the porch, she headed for large double doors and, gazing straight ahead, evaded outstretched hands and plaintive voices. She turned a knob and walked in.

Smells, sounds, and sights assaulted her senses and made her shake with terror. The acrid odor of ammonia hung heavy in the air. She took off her sweater and held it to her nose.

A man in the hallway leaned on crutches, his left leg amputated below the knee, and the gauze covering the stump was caked with dried blood, emitting a rotting odor.

"Help me," he beseeched with a plaintive voice. "My bandage needs changing!"

Tivoli wanted to run, but her feet were rooted in place. Fear, pity, then nausea threatened to overwhelm her. She forced herself to turn and walk into a long room lined with women lying on cots. One sat up and reached an arm to Tivoli. Another lay on her back, moaning, her belly mountained by her advanced pregnancy. By some beds stood racks with bottles of red liquid, rubber hoses channeled to patients' arms. Tivoli saw agony and silent pleas for help in their eyes. She fled from the room. Wanting to scream, she felt drawn, in spite of herself, to the wailing of babies. She entered a ward with cribs and approached a frail child who coughed piteously. The overwhelming stench of feces made her cry out with anger.

How could she help? These people were not real, were they? What could she do for them? Feeling utterly helpless, she tore out of the room, back through the hall, and past the same people occupying the same spaces as before, still wailing and begging for help.

"Help me! It's hot out here! I need water!" called the man from his wheelchair.

Tivoli fled, arriving breathless to where Natasha stood. She leaned against the horse and sobbed, her chest heaving. Fear, anger, and outrage washed over her. And shame – unexplainable shame. She tried to choke back nausea, but finally gave in and vomited into a patch of weeds

Get a grip, she told herself. *I can't go anywhere feeling this way.* She waited ten minutes and felt better. Once back on the horse, she coaxed Natasha to run back along the path, through the meadow, down the hillside through trees, and past the cabin. They trotted along the oceanfront until they reached the familiar painting scene. Tivoli took the horse back to the paddock before running to the wall. Punching the latch, she burst through the opening and into her aunt's sitting room.

Her aunt hurried toward her. "Tivoli! You're ill."

"How would you know?" Tivoli said, anger welling up in her voice. Then noticed a sickening odor, just as Gerard came out of the bedroom carrying a pail and a mop.

"Hope you're feeling better, Miss," he said, with a rueful smile.

Aunt Evelyn led her to the couch. "What happened, child?"

"The hospital." Tivoli glared at the woman. "Tell me about the hospital!"

"You found the Mercy Healing Center? I thought I had hidden that away so well that you would never have to see it!"

"Mercy Healing Center? That's the name? No mercy and no healing exists in that horrible place!"

Aunt Evelyn patted her hand. "Calm down, Tivoli."

Tivoli was breathing hard. "No, I won't. I want to know what that building is and who those people are."

"All right, then. I'd hoped I wouldn't have to tell you about Cora, but it seems I must."

Evelyn clutched a white handkerchief with a tatted border. "Cora." She hesitated. "Cora was Martha's grand niece."

"I already know that."

"Ah, my dear, I'm so sorry that you had to stumble upon that scene. You must relax, or it will be hard for you to hear this story."

Tivoli scowled. "Oh, all right. I'll try."

"Would you like a cup of tea?"

The girl shrugged. "Sure."

"Cora was chosen by her great aunt Martha shortly before that lady died. Cora was a nurse in a hospital at the time. Devoted to her patients, she had no time for, or interest in, Hickory Manor, because she couldn't have given the attention this house needs to keep it going. When Cora's life turned tragic, Martha approached her with the offer."

"Tragic? What happened to her?"

"At the time, no one really knew, except that she became quiet and despondent. Cora kept on with her work, devoted as always, but the sparkle had gone out of her. Martha heard about this and invited the niece to the house with the offer of Hickory Manor. Cora accepted, and after Martha's death, she moved in and quit her job at the hospital."

"How could she stop doing what she loved so much?"

"She didn't really stop, but I'll get to that later. Apparently, she'd fallen hopelessly in love with one of the doctors she worked with, a happily-married man. She wanted to get over her obsession, but the more she tried, the worse it became. She told no one and suffered for years, even thinking of leaving her beloved patients, but she kept on working."

"How sad! Was the doctor aware of her feelings?"

"He must have wondered, but there's no way to know. Martha was close to dying when she asked Cora for help. Martha could still open the lavender door, spend a half hour behind the painting, and then go back to bed again, but she needed someone to take over, and soon. Cora was her last hope, and Cora entered Martha's World each day until Martha died; then the niece moved into the house."

Aunt Evelyn picked up the teapot and re-filled the cups. "Once she became the owner and caretaker of her new domain, Cora set to work. First she created the village and then she built a hospital. She made up patients for that hospital and a manifestation of that same doctor, so that they could live as a married couple."

Tivoli caught her breath. "But that's terrible, Aunt Evelyn!" Then remembered that her great aunt was living a similar fantasy with Morris.

"Not really. Her life was ruined on the outside, but there, for the rest of her life, she could be happy and young once a day, doing the work she loved and loving the man she worked with."

"Why did Cora tell you her story?"

"Because she did not want me to destroy the hospital. I asked her why, and she told me that someday, she might come back and manage it again."

"You mean, after she was dead?"

"Yes. She had reality and fantasy confused. She truly thought that her eternity, Heaven, in other words, would be behind the wall, and she could pick up where she had left off."

Tivoli shuddered. "That sounds crazy."

"It did to me, too, but I've gotten used to her idea. I promised Cora I would keep the hospital. I only went there once and was horrified, so I moved it far away."

"I'm scared to go into Martha's World now," said Tivoli. "Knowing that place is there gives me the creeps."

Aunt Evelyn raised an eyebrow. "The creeps? Must be one of those strange teen-age expressions. Still, it's pretty descriptive, I must admit. I confess it is pretty creepy. You can get rid of it, if you wish. My pledge to Cora doesn't have to apply to you. Just go inside first and take out the patients, then erase the building. That's the way I would do it."

"You mean, kill all those people? I can't do that."

"They're just illusions. You wouldn't be killing them. Just making them disappear."

Tivoli walked home, mulling over the new information about Cora. How could this woman have thrown away a life where she had helped humanity? Wouldn't she eventually have gotten over her feelings for that doctor? Why hadn't she found the courage to move out of town and work in another hospital? Instead, she had not only fantasized a hospital, but had conjured up sick people so that she could make them well, only to have to make more sick people to cure. That was bizarre, totally useless, insane.

But get rid of those people and the hospital? How? Suddenly, she hated it all – the painting, her aunt, Hickory Manor, the trips, the beautiful scenery. Hated and feared Martha's World. Why should she ever go back again? Aunt Evelyn would just have to find another heir.

School started anew, and Tivoli devoted her time to her homework, choir, and band practice. In another year, she would be allowed to join the Clearwater High School Marching Band if she practiced her clarinet faithfully and kept her grades up.

Her parents were relieved. They had heard the Hansens and the O'Learys gossiping about Tivoli's frequent visits to Hickory Manor. *The girl and her family must be after the old place,* they said. But Tivoli had no interest in owning the mansion. She wanted to see the real world and study furniture in other countries, other cultures. She longed to step into actual airplanes and travel far away to experience the world with its smells and squalors and sadness, as well as its magnificence. How could she know what was truly beautiful if she didn't also see the ugly and frightening side of life? How could she ever know joy without experiencing sadness? True, the hospital was ugly and sad, but she could get rid of it, her aunt had reassured her. That was not true in the "real" world, where problems were not easily fixed.

If she came less often, perhaps Aunt Evelyn would choose a different grand niece. Three more cousins had gone to see the Aunt, but Tivoli felt in her heart that none of those girls would inspire friendship with the elderly owner of Hickory Manor.

She visited Gerard when she could, and sometimes she dropped in for tea with Aunt Evelyn. She entered Martha's World only briefly to visit her beloved Natasha and take the horse out for a short ride. She hoped her aunt would get the idea that she was less than enthusiastic about living her life as caretaker of the magic that lay beyond the wall.

The summer before her Senior year, Tivoli found a job at Jacobsen's Antique Furniture Store. She loved the work and commented on different styles and finishes. The Jacobsens were amazed at her knowledge of furniture, and encouraged Tivoli to help in the refinishing shop.

During the following school year, she continued working on Saturdays.

After graduation, she began full-time employment at Jacobsen's, and one day, a new person came to work at the store.

Barry.

In spite of many freckles and reddish-gold, unruly hair, Barry's face was tanned. So were the muscular legs that showed beneath the khaki shorts with many pockets. He was wearing a bright yellow long-sleeved shirt.

Tivoli could hardly wait to go to work the following morning, so she could see Barry again. For several days, she watched as Mr. Jacobsen trained him on the sales floor. She was impressed by his confidence and easy manner with customers. He now wore slacks, and each day, a different shirt in a bright color – blue, orange, purple. The clothes enhanced his vibrant personality.

Tivoli looked forward to seeing him each day, and by the end of the week, she knew she was in love.

His friendliness was disarming, and she soon lost the feeling of awe. They talked during lunch breaks and went for walks after work. She sometimes invited him home for dinner, and her parents enjoyed talking to him. By the end of the summer, she thought of him as her best friend.

Barry entered his second year at Nashville State College and hoped to major in geology at Colorado State. During her senior year, they started dating, mostly going on day hikes in the Smoky Mountains, where Barry taught her rock climbing skills. He offered to teach her how to drive, but she told him she had no interest in driving, unless she owned her own car.

Tivoli couldn't imagine her life without Barry. She knew much about his life and she had told him a great deal about herself, but sooner or later, she would have to introduce him to Hickory Manor.

She took him to meet Gerard, and they walked through the rooms of furniture, while she shared her love and knowledge of antiques. Gerard was warm and welcoming, as usual, but Barry said he felt uncomfortable with Aunt Evelyn.

"I'm not much of a tea drinker, especially out of dainty little cups. I didn't know what to do with my big paws, and I felt as though that old lady was sizing me up."

Tivoli laughed. "She was, and I know her well enough to think that you passed the test. She likes intelligent people who carry on good conversations, and she seemed genuinely interested in your excavation trips to Utah and Colorado."

"She does seem to know a lot, and apparently has been all over the world."

Tivoli smiled to herself and said, "Hmmm, in a manner of speaking."

Two days later, when she arrived home from work, her mother met her at the door.

"Gerard called a few minutes ago and wants you to come immediately. Aunt Evelyn is ill."

CHAPTER SEVEN

While her mother backed the car out of the garage, Tivoli's mind raced with dread. Underneath her concern for Aunt Evelyn lay a fear of what the elderly woman's illness would mean in Tivoli's life.

Her mother patted her knee. "Come on, relax, honey," she soothed. She probably just wants your company. Gerard can take perfectly good care of her, I'm sure,"

"I guess so. Maybe she just needs somebody besides Gerard to help her. I know where all her photo albums are, the *National Geographic* magazines, and other travel books. We can look at them together, which we often do, and maybe it will make her feel better."

But Tivoli knew that she alone could keep Martha's World alive and whole. She kissed her mother's cheek and jumped out of the car. "See you later!" she said, with a cheeriness she did not feel.

Gerard met her at the door. "I'm so glad you could come right away, Tivoli. She's taken to bed and is very weak. It's probably just a flu."

"I've always wondered, Gerard, why you don't go inside Martha's World."

"Oh, I suppose I could, Miss. I just don't have the ability to change anything."

"Why not?"

"Your Aunt has never volunteered to teach me, and besides, I think the whole idea of the place is very strange. I prefer the world on this side of that wall!"

Tivoli studied his eyes as he spoke. It was the first time she had ever heard Gerard criticize anything about her aunt, or her aunt's life. "I feel that way, too, sometimes, but so much of it is beautiful and interesting. How long has Aunt Evelyn been ill?"

"Since yesterday, but she hasn't gone inside Martha's World for two days."

Gerard led her through Aunt Evelyn's parlor, around the painted wall, and, for her first time, she entered the bedroom. It was stuffier than the sitting room and felt moist because of the vaporizer that steamed from a corner.

Aunt Evelyn reached out her hand, and Tivoli took it in both of hers, studying the wan face against propped-up pillows. The woman's eyes lacked their usual sparkle.

"How are you feeling, Aunt Evelyn?"

Her aunt fished a Kleenex out of a box on her bed and coughed. "Not well, but it's only a head cold. I hardly ever get sick, so when I do, I feel like I'm dying. I'm sure I'll be fine in a few days, or at least, well enough to recuperate somewhere: the village, maybe, or the small town near Buenos Aires. Perhaps you can go with me."

"That sounds lovely, Aunt, but first, we have to get you well."

"Child, I haven't been inside Martha's World for a few days. I don't know what shape it will be in. Can you see what you can do?" She took the key chain from around her neck and gave it to Tivoli.

Tivoli clutched the key, aware of the woman's trust. She walked around to the sitting room, opened the lock in the painting, and walked through. As it slid in place behind her, her feet sank into spongy earth – not wet, like mud, but soft. With each step, she had to suck her feet out of ankle-deep matter.

Better stop. Repair from here. She willed her mind to calm down, then focus, un-focus, and focus again on something easy and close – the lavender around her. The blooms became more brilliant, and the ground under her feet, firmer. But the inlet in the distance blurred in a smear of color that blended with the woods beyond. The weird, frightening landscape reminded her of Turner's later impressionistic paintings: beautiful, but not a world for walking or comfort. The distortion inside Martha's World scared her, and she wanted to flee the challenge, but she knew she must try to do her best to repair the scene.

She worried about Natasha and Stallion. There was no way she could walk around the corner to the paddock until she had stabilized the foreground landscape. Aunt Evelyn had told her that once the painting scene had been reconstructed to its basic form, all other places would be fine and would not need touching up. .

Tivoli found a rock and sat down. The blurring of colors made her feel dizzy. She closed her eyes for a moment, then opened them and focused on the water, until it looked natural and lapped up against the beach with small, regular waves. Her gaze settled on the trees beyond, until she could see individual branches and stems. The restoration process became easier as she continued. Soon, the grass looked naturally green. The breeze, which had whooped like a stretched-out audio tape, warping the sound with strange waves of high and low, became normal and felt soft and cool as before. The sun's rays flowed warm and constant. Martha's World worked again, as it had for 160 years, and she exhaled a breath of relief.

Tivoli got up and followed the wall to the edge, went around the corner, and saw the village. It looked normal and bright. She kept walking until she came to the pasture. When she called to the mare, Natasha sauntered toward her.

"Hello, girl. Did you feel it, too?" The horse extended her neck toward Tivoli to be scratched. Tivoli pulled a sprig of lavender from her pocket, and Natasha munched sleepily. "I'll be back soon, and then we'll ride again."

Tivoli ran back to the wall, feeling firm ground beneath her feet, and walked through the opening into the living room and around to the bedroom.

She told Aunt Evelyn that she had repaired Martha's World, and promised to be back the next day.

A week later, her aunt, now fully recovered, asked Tivoli to come to discuss important business. Tivoli dreaded the visit. As she walked up the stairs, she felt that these would be her last truly free moments. For, though she did not want the responsibility of Hickory Manor, she knew she would say yes. Aunt Evelyn needed an heir, and she was the logical choice.

When Gerard escorted Tivoli into the parlor, Aunt Evelyn handed her the customary cup of tea, then sat in the wing-backed chair, head bent.

"I'm getting on in years. My recent illness was a warning that I need to choose the person to whom I want to leave all my worldly possessions," Aunt Evelyn smiled, "and even my not-so-worldly ones!" she added.

"Hickory Manor will always need an owner who understands its true value, which to me and my predecessors is the life that thrives beyond these walls. The house itself is probably badly in need of repairs. I don't know much about that, and I've never cared, as long as I could live comfortably in these few rooms, stay warm and dry, and have enough to eat. It would be expensive to renovate, and if someone did away with Martha's painting, then, of course, everything Martha, Cora and I have created over all these years would be lost forever."

Tivoli shifted her weight on the couch and crossed her arms.

Her aunt caught her breath, then resumed. "Only you, my dear Tivoli, of all my nieces, have shown a genuine interest in her old Aunt, even before you knew about the mural. I appreciate that and I enjoy your company. You have the ability to create inside Martha's World and understand its value."

"And I love much of it, Aunt Evelyn. It's always with me in my mind, wherever I go."

"I'm glad, but if you and Barry are serious about marriage some day, he needs to know about this. You must take him inside and show him around. He will be only the second man who has ever been on the other side of the painting. The other was Morris, before he went into the Service."

"What if Barry doesn't want anything to do with it?" Tivoli asked.

"You can still both live here. He could have a job; extra money to fix up the place would be helpful. He doesn't have to tie himself to the house. He'd be free to travel, as long as you were around daily to visit Martha's World."

"But Aunt Evelyn! What if I want to travel with him?"

"You can, my dear. You can create anywhere in the world right here! All you need is travel books and your own rich imagination, and you and Barry could have a glorious time, yet be able to sleep in your own bed every night."

Tivoli thought about the magical world, so easily available – a realm of music and travel, perfect weather, beautiful scenery. Barry could ride Stallion while she rode Natasha. Together, they could go anywhere.

She remembered Barry telling her about his trip the previous summer, visiting a cave with stalactites, finding feldspar rocks on the cave floor. But also, being caught in a storm with rain falling in torrents so that the rocky territory he was climbing became slippery and treacherous.

Tivoli mentioned Barry's love of rock hunting.

"Come with me." Evelyn led the way into Martha's World and transformed herself into her Evvy personality, this time wearing hiking boots.

"We need to design boots for you, so you can help create an entirely new environment. In fact, let's take the horses, so we can feel as though we are deep into wild country!"

Her aunt led the way on Stallion, creating horse trails as she went and leading them through a more mountainous terrain. When at last she stopped, they were at the edge of an inky abyss, familiar to Tivoli as a new canvas – a blank space onto which they could project a scene.

"I'll start," said Evvy, and she squinted her eyes until, with some effort, she had built a volcanic mountain.

"Wow! That looks like pictures I've seen of Mount St. Helens, the inside of the crater with the dome that keeps building up."

"Yes, that's it. We can start with this, and you may want to add areas that are rich in geodes, and a stream for panning gold, nickel, galena, or whatever you wish!"

Tivoli gazed in awe. This would look like Paradise to Barry! Everything he could ever want, and all in one place. "I could build him a laboratory, where he can create for testing, and I'll set up shelves to display the rock specimens he finds in Little Himalayas!!"

"I'll leave you now, and you can create on your own. Come back whenever you're ready. Then, you can think about when you want to bring in Barry."

Her aunt left and Tivoli remained, alone in the new, startlingly diversified terrain. She sat atop Natasha a long time, staring at the crags and pinnacles of granite and basalt. Was it too perfect? How could all of this be in one place? If she could just spread the scene out, to make it less accessible and harder to reach. The real excitement of a geological dig was the scarcity of precious ores. Here, the challenge was missing. Everything seemed too easy.

Would Barry be impressed? A fear loomed in her that he might not like this at all. She jumped off the horse and wandered through rock formations. High up on the promontory, she noticed something sparkling brilliantly in the sun. Crystal? How could she possibly reach it?

Tivoli began to climb but the wall was steep, and she had to look for handholds, as Barry had taught her the previous summer. Only then she had been roped up to him, and he had pounded pitons into walls and attached a rope with carabiners. Without him, she wasn't sure how this equipment could help, and she had no idea in her mind how to form these tools. Besides, fear kept her from being able to concentrate on creating anything. So she searched carefully and found ledges for her feet, as she pulled herself up with her hands.

Tivoli kept telling herself this world was not real, and yet, the exertion was just as exhausting as the climbing she had done in the Smoky Mountains. She looked down into a ravine and felt instant panic. A rock beneath her foot gave way, and she stumbled, landing with a thud on an outcrop of boulders. Knowing she had to turn back, she hung on with her hands and inched her way along the ledge, searching for footholds, feeling nauseous with fear. She found a place for her right foot, but when she trusted her weight on the narrow lip of earth, it, too, crumbled.

She tried to envision a new ledge, but fear kept her from being able to create a firm place to put her feet. Her body lurched, and her legs dangled in mid-air while her fingers clutched the edge of boulders.

The hold seemed solid, but Tivoli knew she didn't have the strength in her fingers to hang on. She tried to hoist herself up, but realized there was no place for her feet. Could she actually die if she fell from this precipice?

No! Tivoli's mind screamed. *Build another ledge! I can do it!* But her fingers cramped. She could no longer hold on.

She felt herself falling, falling....

CHAPTER EIGHT

"Water! Now!" Tivoli screamed. She had no time to look down, or to focus, only to visualize a deep pool below with a soft bottom.

Too late to inhale, she held her nose, clamping her mouth shut as her body sliced through water, and she felt intense pressure in her head. Her feet touched bottom and, flexing her knees, Tivoli pushed herself off the slippery clay and broke through the surface. Letting go of her nose, she sputtered and coughed.

Tivoli's panic subsided and she looked around her. The pool, a perfect circle, was surrounded by a steep bank of dark gray clay. Treading water, she focused on a section of the bank until she created a sandy beach and a clearing and swam toward it. She tried to make a shallow section near this, so she could climb out, but realized she had no clear picture in her mind of how to accomplish that. She dug her hands into the clay beach and hoisted herself out of the pond, her boots heavy with water and mud.

She scrambled through thinned-out bush, her shoes squishing, and stumbled toward the grassy spot where she had left Natasha. She took off her shoes, stuffed her wet socks inside, and, tying the strings together, hung them around the mare's neck. Weary and sore, she climbed onto her horse. Tivoli knew that once she entered the living room, the shoes and her clothes would be dry. All the water and mud would abe left behind in Martha's World.

She shivered as she rode Natasha to the paddock and then walked back toward the wall. Had she really been close to losing her life? Why had she been able to create that pool so quickly? Always before, it had taken at least several minutes to manifest a scene, or to alter something. But her desire had been so strong, so desperate, that her mind's focus had been laser-sharp and powerful. She recalled having no doubt at all, just an immediate assurance that the pool would be there.

With great relief, she entered the sitting room. Her aunt eyed her with curiosity and concern, but Tivoli, shaken by the experience, was anxious to leave. She said goodbye and sped home.

She waited a week before returning, struggling with conflicting thoughts of staying in her own familiar world or going back into this new terrain she was building. She realized it had been her fear that had created the crisis, and her determination to survive that had saved her.

And had she not reached the point beyond being able to go back on her promise to take care of Martha's World and Hickory Manor? Her aunt trusted her and had no alternate person to take over the responsibility.

She finally called Gerard and arranged for a visit with Aunt Evelyn. As they sipped tea, she explained her near accident, and her fear that she might have died. She even confessed the burden she felt about the inheritance.

"Ah, my dear, I remember those doubts well after I had promised Cora. Whether or not any of us could have died in Martha's World, well, this has never been tested, so I couldn't tell you. But I assure you, I have never regretted my decision to live the life that I have for all these years."

Tivoli's enthusiasm returned in the weeks that followed, as she and Evvy added to the new terrain, which they named *Little Himalayas*. They built a railroad track and added a three-car train that meandered through magnificent scenery. They expanded the area into many different scenic panoramas and a huge variety of rock formations, ready to be excavated.

Aunt Evelyn urged her to bring Barry and introduce him to Martha's World, but Tivoli couldn't bring herself to tell him about it.

One day, Barry called and asked her to dress for a special evening. He brought her twelve long-stemmed roses and drove to Henri's Cuisine, a luxurious restaurant overlooking the Tennessee River. They snuggled together in a booth with tall sides. His excitement bordered on nervousness that she pretended not to notice. When the waiter poured a golden bubbly beverage from a large bottle, Barry lifted his glass in a toast.

"Champaigne?" Tivoli asked.

"Not in this state, youngster! You're only twenty. Ginger ale is about the closest look-alike I could think of."

"Thanks, old man. Why, you practically have one foot in the grave!" Tivoli shot back, clinking her glass against his.

Barry reached into his pocket. He took out a small box and handed it to her.

Tivoli inspected the maroon box, turning it over and feeling the smooth texture.

"Well, open it," Barry said, putting an arm around her.

Tivoli snapped open the cover. Inside, a deep red ruby in a white gold setting sat perched on a velvet cushion.

His hand trembled as it grasped hers and the box. She looked up and saw distress on his face.

"I – I – I," he stammered. "I had a speech all ready, but, but, Oh, well I mean, will you marry me?"

Tivoli leaned over to kiss him, realizing that she had also been rehearsing an answer to the question she had secretly anticipated all evening. "Oh, Barry, Of course I want to. I think about that all the time these days. And now tonight, the roses, the ring, and the ginger ale." She smiled, stifling a chuckle. "One of these days, I'll tell you a story about ginger ale. Yes, I'll marry you!"

Barry wrapped her in his arms, just as she heard strains of a violin, coming closer. She recognized an Elvis song: *Fools Rush In*. The violinist approached their table, and

Barry sang along, "But I can't help falling in love with you!" People at nearby tables clapped and smiled.

The evening was balmy, and the quarter moon, a crisp sliver over the river. They clasped hands while they walked, Neither wanted to talk but savored in silence the trust they felt with each other.

Her parents feigned surprise when she showed them the ring the next morning. Then told her that they had already suspected that Barry had "popped the question," because he had visited them a week earlier, to ask their permission. They had been impressed and touched by this rather old-fashioned formality, and they had given him their hearty blessing.

The discussed the wedding, but decided to wait until Tivoli had spent at least a year at Nashville State College, and Barry would come home from Colorado as often as he could.

"After we're married, you could transfer to Colorado State for your Sophomore year, and we could be together again," Barry suggested.

Tivoli didn't know how to tell him that this would be impossible, because of Hickory Manor.

On Saturdays, they drove for miles to rock quarries and sections of the river where they could hunt for unusual rocks. In her mind, Tivoli kept seeing the limitless variety in the Little Himalayas.

She told Aunt Evelyn about her desire to go to Nashville State in the fall, and said she would try her best to come home each day and enter Martha's World.

"Why not take one of those on-line courses I keep hearing about?" Aunt Evelyn suggested.

"Not the same. I want to be able to get acquainted with other students and experience the that college atmosphere."

Her aunt had no more comments about the subject, but Tivoli suspected that she was afraid Tivoli would not be able to take care of Martha's World property, if this became necessary while she was going through her college year.

She visited Aunt Evelyn and Gerard when she could, and one day, when they were having tea, her aunt said, "You have become skilled at creating in Martha's World."

Tivoli looked up, wondering where her aunt was heading with that remark. "Thank you, Aunt Evelyn, but you are much better at it than I am."

"You'll learn even more, with practice. I must tell you that I have finalized my will, and I am leaving you the house and an inheritance that should last you for many years."

Tivoli had dreaded this anticipated conversation, and said, "But Aunt, suppose Barry doesn't want to live here? Is there no one else?"

"No, you are the only person I would leave it to. And I'm convinced he'll be thrilled with the world we have created for him!"

Tivoli hoped so, but was unsure that she wanted the responsibility. Reluctantly, she said, "I'll do my best, Aunt Evelyn. For you."

"Good, Tivoli. And now I have a special request. Since you have become so good at creating people, as well as objects, I wonder if you could bring me back as young Evvy after I die. I'm not sure how well that would work, or even if I would ever know, but Morris already lives there and is very real to me, so we could be together."

Tivoli shivered, as a feeling of horror washed over her. "I don't know, Aunt Evelyn. Is that possible? If I did that, wouldn't you be merely something out of my imagination, like Natasha?"

"I have no way of knowing, of course," said Aunt Evelyn. "But will you try? I would be much comforted if you told me you would attempt to do this. If I have your word, I know I can trust you."

With reluctance, Tivoli promised her aunt that she would honor her request.

One Sunday evening, when she and Barry returned from a day in the mountains, her mother met her at the door. "We received sad news, dear. Aunt Evelyn died early this morning in her sleep."

Tivoli breath caught in her throat and she brought her hands to her face. "Oh, Mom, no!"

Her mother hugged her. 'I'm sorry, darling. Gerard asked us to send you as soon as you came home, no matter what time it was. I don't understand the urgency, but he seemed adamant about it."

"I'll take you there," Barry said. "Would you like me to go in with you?"

"I appreciate the ride, but I need to go in alone. I'll call Dad when I'm ready to come home."

In Barry's van, Tivoli broke down and sobbed, her love for Aunt Evelyn mingling with fear for her own future. Although she had thought about this many times since her last conversation with the elderly woman, she had hoped that Aunt Evelyn would live many years and perhaps even find a new heir for her property.

Approaching Hickory Manor, she noticed a coroner's van. Barry folded her in his arms, and she cried on his shoulder, kissed him quickly and hurried out of the car. She walked past the long, slim hearse and up the steps. Gerard met her, calm as always, but without his usual smile.

"She's still on her bed, Miss Tivoli. I wanted you to see her before they take her away."

Tivoli followed him. "How did she die?"

"A stroke, the doctor says. She went peacefully. She visited Martha's World just yesterday afternoon. The last days were difficult for her. She was weak and I think she knew that she was dying. She stayed in bed, except to step through the painting, but it took a great deal of effort. Yesterday, she was still lucid and told me that when she died, I was to call you right away."

Tivoli stood by her aunt's bedside. The inert face looked placid and totally serene. Tivoli let the tears flow once more.

"I'll watch over the place, Aunt Evelyn," she whispered. "And I'll do what needs to be done."

The director entered the room. "We'll take her now, Miss Hansen. You may want to step into the kitchen with Gerard."

Tea was ready in the breakfast nook. Gerard sat across from Tivoli and took hold of her hands. "She loved you very much, Tivoli. You have made her life happy these last years. She was less lonely."

"But I must be here every day now, to keep Martha's World going. I dread the responsibility."

Gerard fished into his jacket pocket and pulled out the key chain. The tiny instrument that would enable her to go inside the painting any time, gleamed in the light of the breakfast nook. He handed the chain to her, and she placed it around her neck.

After the hearse left with Aunt Evelyn's body, Tivoli wandered around the gloomy room that she had so often visited in the past.

This room is one thing I'm going to change when the place is really mine. I'm going to open windows, let in sunlight, and paint the other walls. I'll buy new furniture and get rid of those heavy drapes.

She stood for a moment, staring at the mural she knew so well, then opened the latch in the wall. She walked through to the meadow, realizing that her aunt was not behind her, nor waiting in the sitting room for her to come back. Would she honor Aunt Evelyn's request? No, not yet. She needed to be alone now. Better to wait until after the funeral.

Find Morris? That seemed too strange. What would she tell him? Would he, an illusion, understand anything at all?

The funeral took place in the Clearwater Community hall and drew a capacity crowd. Family mourners, as well as curiosity seekers, filed by the open casket that displayed the trim, groomed body of the family matriarch. For many, it was the first time they had ever seen the much-fabled resident of Hickory Manor.

Tivoli's eyes welled up with tears as she stared at the smile on the beloved face and the bloom that looked so natural on the elderly cheeks.

CHAPTER NINE

Aunt Evelyn's lawyer summoned Tivoli and her parents to his office to read the will. Tivoli was the sole heir to Evelyn O'Leary's fortune, which consisted of Hickory Manor, three acres of wooded property with a clearing for the lavender plants, and enough investments to last, figuring in interest, for at least forty years. There was not enough money to improve the place, only to cover maintenance and Tivoli's personal needs.

Although Tivoli knew she should be making plans to occupy the Manor, she told Barry that she wanted to wait until after the wedding, when they could both move in together. He promised to use his own earnings to fix up the place, room by room, and to improve the outside. "With any luck," he told her, "if we can get the house back to its good solid condition, we could sell it!"

Tivoli felt distressed, not knowing how to answer. She went to the mansion every day now, at least long enough to enter the painting, and to talk briefly to Gerard, who kept the place spotlessly clean and always had a warm meal or a snack waiting for her.

A week after she officially took over Hickory Manor, she decided to honor Aunt Evelyn's request. She entered the painting and sat on the rock at the edge of the lavender. She willed her mind to calm down enough to create Evvy's image. The people she had designed up to now had come through as a mere outline first, and she had worked on them until they each looked unique and had personalities. To create someone that she had known on the outside seemed more difficult, but that is how each of her predecessors had made up their lovers.

She focused, un-focused, focused again, until a woman began to take form. She imagined her image of Evvy. Gradually, she saw the auburn hair, the vivacious smile, a calf-length skirt, sweater, bobby socks, and saddle shoes. Then, the face came into focus, and Evvy walked toward her.

Fearful, Tivoli took a step backwards, but Evvy's smile was so reassuring, that she smiled back.

"Tivoli! You did it! You created me in Martha's World."

Tivoli took a sharp breath. Had she really brought her aunt back to life in here? Was Aunt Evelyn actually remembering her request, grateful to her for complying? Or was she herself making all of this up?

"I'm off now, to find Morris," Evvy said, waving. "Tally-ho!"

"Bye-bye," Tivoli called.

She left the mural quickly, disturbed by how easy this had been. The following days, she visited the village often, always running into Evvy and Morris. Evvy seemed to know all about the inheritance and her own funeral. And she asked about Barry.

"When are you going to bring your friend in here and introduce us?"

Tivoli knew she had to take that step, but had no intention of letting him know about the people she had created. She couldn't imagine introducing him to Evvy or Morris.

When Barry asked her to join him and his climbing group in on a four-day dig, she knew she had to tell him about Hickory Manor, about the three owners before her, about the painting. The trip would not be for a month, so she would hold off on telling him about needing to be at the mansion every day. Hopefully, by then, he might understand. For now, she said she needed to think about his offer.

She invited him out for coffee, and explained this aspect of her life for the past seven years. He listened in silence, and she felt a moment of panic in the pit of her stomach.

"How could you have hidden this from me?" Barry said, and she sensed his anger. "All those times I tried to reach you, and you didn't answer your phone. I always wondered, but figured you were helping your mother, or in the car. Or you were just visiting with your aunt and had your phone turned off."

"I didn't know how to tell you. I was afraid you would think it was crazy, or that I loved that place more than you." Tivoli felt a lump in her throat, but didn't want to cry.

"Well, do you? Is that place more important than our relationship?"

"No, of course not. Please, will you give me a chance to show you what's behind that wall?"

Barry didn't answer and was quiet while he drove her home. She tried to start a conversation, but didn't know how.

When he stopped the car in front of her house. His hands clutched the steering wheel and he stared straight ahead. "I need some time to think about this. I love you so much, but I feel betrayed."

She reached for his hand. "I guess I see your point. I had never even thought about that, but if the tables were turned, I think I would feel the same way."

He gave her a short kiss, and she stepped out of the car.

She could hardly sleep that night, and the next day, she went through the motions of going through the portal and visiting the horses, but her heart was elsewhere. She felt abandoned and fearful.

Barry called three days later. "I've let it sink in, and I'm willing to give the place a try. Will you forgive me for being angry with you?"

Tivoli felt her heart beating fast, and she breathed a sigh of relief. "Of course, dear! I've missed you. Can you come this afternoon?"

He drove her to the mansion, and she led him into the sitting room. She explained the wall to him, pleased that he was so fascinated by the fan door in the lavender scene. When she opened it with the tiny key, she could hear his breath catch.

"It's all right," she said, taking his hand. "You'll love this!" She pulled him through the opening and it closed behind them.

Barry stood staring, amazement in his eyes.

"How do we get out of here?"

Tivoli laughed. "Same way we came in. Only we won't need a key this time."

Barry looked back at the wall. "This is crazy. Are we still on Earth, or on a different planet?"

"Relax. It's all right. It's really great. You'll see."

She walked him to the beach. They took off their shoes and socks and waded into the water and back to the warm sand. She took him to the paddock and introduced him to Stallion, Natasha, and a half dozen other horses that grazed placidly.

Barry followed her with nervous excitement, rubbing his hands through his sandy-red curls. "What's happening? Is this real? Are you real?" He pinched her arm.

"Ouch! Yes, I'm real," Tivoli laughed, feeling proud and encouraged by his enthusiasm. "Unbelievable isn't it? And there's more. Much, much more! Only let's go back out, so you know that's possible. You need time to think about all of this."

"I'll say, I need to think about it!" Barry told her when they were back relaxing in the sitting room.

As they drove home, Barry said, "That is the weirdest experience I've ever had, but strangely wonderful, too. Does Gerard know about it?"

"Well, somewhat. Why don't you talk to him?"

Barry came back several times in the next few weeks and had long conversations with Gerard, following him around from room to room, admiring the furniture.

"I can see why you love this place so much," he told Tivoli. "That furniture is beautiful and priceless. Think what that could do for us when we decide to sell some of it. We could use the money to fix up Hickory Manor, put money away for our kids' education, and buy us a whole lot of equipment for our digs!"

Tivoli took a deep breath. "But that's Gerard's. His personal property. It is not ours to do with what we want."

"Well, I thought that Gerard sort of came with the house," Barry said. "Its indentured servant, so to speak. He has no other job but this. It's his whole life."

"But Barry,he's talented. He could go anywhere, and repair or deal in furniture. He certainly has the ability."

"At his age? Think, Tivoli. But I've been curious about that Martha's World. I think I'm ready to go back inside, if you'll take me."

Tivoli led him through, and they walked to the paddock to saddle up Natasha and Stallion. They rode to the opposite side of the inlet, around to the ocean to the cabin, and dismounted to go inside. Tivoli led Barry through the fragrant cedar-paneled living room to the winding staircase. Once they reached the loft, Tivoli walked to the window.

Barry stood behind her, his arms encircling her body. "What a view! It truly looks and sounds like the ocean."

He turned to look at the queen-sized brass bed with its colorful star quilt. "We certainly don't need to go far for our honeymoon! Let's try out the bed. See if it's strong enough to hold up under vigorous exercise!"

She squirmed in his arms, and glanced up at him with a coy smile. "Barry!" She tugged at his hand and pulled him back toward the staircase. "I think we should wait until the honeymoon, as you suggested."

"Oh, well, hope springs eternal," Barry laughed.

" I'll have to work on that bed so it will stand up to any earthquake we might create."

They remounted the horses and Tivoli rode ahead through the woods. When they came to a clearing, she turned aside to allow Barry, atop Stallion, to get the full scope of the panorama.

She watched as his eyes grew big. "Unbelievable! Like the inside of Mount Saint Helens!"

"That's the idea. Aunt Evelyn used that model in her mind, and we both created the rest. Let me show you!"

They rode the horses to the bottom of a steep outcrop, then dismounted and started climbing the rocky terrain until they reached the crest and looked down.

"Geodes! In the crater of St. Helen's? Igneous rock. Sedimentary rock. All in one place? How could this be? It's – it's impossible."

Tivoli felt excited and pleased. Barry was like a enchanted child in a newly-discovered toy land.

"That river shimmers! But not just from the sun," Barry said.

Tivoli pointed. "If you look closely, you'll notice nuggets of gold. And there's silver and galena close by, too."

"Let's collect what we can and tomorrow, come back with sacks for carrying."

"Not necessary. Come with me." She led him to the lab, set up with a microscope, chemicals, and slides, as well as pick axes, hammers, and gold pans. "You don't have to take it anywhere. Look. Bunsen burners, a rock tumbler, an oven. And shelves for storage and display."

"But that's half the fun, showing and sharing with my friends. I can hardly wait to tell them. They don't have to know where it came from!"

"It doesn't work that way. You'll see. But you can have everything right here, and I can even create your rock-hound friends for you!"

Barry was silent when they brought the horses back. He took her hand as they walked back to the wall. "It's all a dream. I can't wait to go back in there again soon."

"It's waiting for us," Tivoli said, as they left Martha's World and were once more seated in the living room.

Barry reached into his pockets, and smiled ruefully. "Empty. I stuffed some of those gold nuggets in here, but they're gone. I guess crime doesn't pay. I'm supposed to leave it all in Martha's World."

She told him about her shoe and the shell she had tried to take out after her first visit. "I wanted to take in carrots for Natasha, but that didn't work, either. So I created a fruit able stand, and I can bring the horses treats any th.

"Well, no matter. It's great fun. A geologist's Disney World. I feel bone-tired from all that climbing we did this afternoon. And we don't have to pay for food or lodging, or anything. Bless your ancient Aunt Martha, and her great, imaginative longing."

Tivoli went to bed that night, pleased, and relieved. Little Himalayas had passed the test. Now if she could just convince Barry that Hickory Manor was the perfect home!

In the next few months, Barry joined her several times to journey to far-away places behind the mural. He enjoyed the excursions, but his mind was on the anticipated four-day climb in Bryce Canyon.

"What about it, Tiv? You haven't given me your answer yet. Are you coming this us to Utah?"

Iivoli hesitated, averting her eyes away from his probing stare. "I can't, Barry. I need to stay here."

"Of course you can. Take some time off from Hickory Manor. Gerard is there, and he does all of the work, anyway."

Tivoli plopped down on the couch, and held her cell phone close to her ear, hoping her mother was not within earshot. "But we can spend those days here! I can create a canyon, and we can explore that. And we can sleep in our own beds at night, instead of in a drafty tent."

"What? Come on, Tivoli. You can't be serious. You love camping and traveling."

She could sense his irritation,, and it alarmed her. "I do! But now that Aunt Evelyn is gone, I can't leave the Manor. Something will happen if I do." Reluctantly, she told him about the instability of Martha's World if it was not tended each day.

"Well, then, leave it. You don't need that place to be happy, do you?"

Tivoli's tried to control her voice. "No-o-o-, of course not, but..."

"But nothing. You have the furniture, and all your expertise. Thanks to Gerard, you can cane any chair as well as he can, and you can refinish any piece to its original beauty. That, in itself, is treasure enough."

She felt her temper flare. "You mean, don't go into Martha's World? Is that what you're saying? I thought you liked it!"

She heard Barry's sigh. "Tivoli, Bryce Canyon changes, and yet is eternal. It's been there for eons, and that's its magic. An earth tremor can change an entire mountain in a few seconds, and no human has the power to stop the wrath of Nature. It can rain and storm and be downright nasty and dangerous, but that's the beauty of rock climbing and spelunking and searching for treasure.

"That world of yours, Martha's world, it's fun, it's outrageously ingenious, like Disneyland in mid-America, but it isn't...*real*!"

CHAPTER TEN

Tivoli snapped her phone shut as angry tears welled up in her eyes. The secret life she had lived for the past six years, her fear of introducing Martha's World to him, the care she had taken, her preparation, her longing to have him be part of her world, and he trivialized it in three short words, *It isn't real!* Well, let him go to Utah without her. Maybe when he came back, he would see things differently.

But different how? She was startled by that thought. Deep inside her, she feared he was right. Of course Martha's World wasn't real. But then, no vacation was actually real because every escapade took you away from a life of responsibility and suspended you in a world of make believe, to be savored later in your mind.

In the days following that phone call with Barry, Tivoli spent hours in Martha's World, riding Natasha, or resting in her cabin, drinking coffee in the village with Evvy and Morris and their friends. She re-designed the laboratory and introduced clouds, rain, and strong winds into the virtual memory base. She packed the hills behind the village with new snow, built a ski shop, and skied until exhausted. She listened to the "William Tell Overture" and taught it to the orchestra, segment by segment.

Yet now that she could be there for as long as she wanted and could have anything she wished, the longing to step into the painting began to lose some of its potency.

Barry was the only person that Tivoli had been able to share this with, besides Aunt Evelyn and Gerard. And they took this world so for granted that she had never discussed any misgivings with them.

When Barry returned from Utah, he took her out for lunch. "Tiv, I've been thinking."

She didn't like the tone of that.

"I do not want to live in Hickory Manor. And since you feel that you must, that's a conflict."

"But we could have a house in town, too. I'll be in the mansion during the day. Gerard can take care of it just fine at night."

"No, Tivoli. That won't do. I missed you on this last trip. You've gone with us before, and we always have fun together. I will continue to go on digs and climbs, and I want very much to share them with you. So I'm giving you a choice, darling. Hickory Manor – or me!"

Tivoli felt numb. "I need some time to think," she whispered.

"Of course you do. You might even want to discuss it with Gerard."

Yes, she would confide in Gerard. And she would go into Martha's World to visit her favorite places with Evvy and Morris and tend to the horses. From that, would come her answer.

The next day, when she stepped through the painting, she sat for a long time on a rock at the edge of the lavender patch and breathed in the flowery fragrance. She willed the rain to fall gently and drops splattered on her hands and cheeks. She walked to the village and met Evvy and Morris, both of them with wet clothes plastered to their bodies and dripping hair.

"What are you doing?" Evvy demanded. "Where does all of this rain come from?"

Tivoli could not recall a time that Evvy, or even her aunt, had used such a harsh tone. The same question plagued Tivoli that had haunted her ever since she had created Evvy. Was that really her great aunt talking, or her creation, with the thoughts she had put there? Was she projecting this irritation on Evvy? She would never be sure.

She thought of going to her Aunt's favorite place by Ayers Rock, but had no real desire to do so, or to go anywhere else. All she wanted was to step back out through the painting and curl up in the breakfast nook, talking to Gerard, the eternal pot of tea between them.

When she left the painting, she headed for the kitchen and explained her misgivings to Gerard. He smiled. "Ah, Miss Tivoli! You are the first to ever have doubts about that place. I congratulate you!"

"Congratulate me? But why? I feel like a traitor. This is such a great gift, and now I'm not sure if I want it."

"But your Barry. Surely he is a greater gift. I'm very fond of your young man."

Gerard leaned over and held her hands, looking into her eyes. "Miss Tivoli, would you like my advice?"

Tivoli nodded.

"Then get out. Go away. Build your future with Barry before it is too late. The others never figured that out, and they threw away their lives. I have so hoped and prayed that you would not do the same!"

Tivoli stared at him. "You mean, give up Hickory Manor?"

"Yes, give up Hickory Manor. Let's walk around outside the house, and I'll point out all the things that are wrong with it. It will take years, much time, and much money, to make this place look like anything but a decrepit old structure. I don't know what you might want to do with the property, but you'd be better off if you just tear it down and build anew."

"But Gerard, you know what happens to Martha's World if I don't tend to it."

"Yes, of course. In seven days, it would be beyond repair and in ten, it would be completely gone."

"Can't you go in there?"

Gerard shook his head and gave her a wistful smile. "No, I can't, Miss Tivoli."

"Why not?"

"I just can't. Trust my word, for now."

"What will happen to you? Where will you go? What will you do? This place has been your whole life. You're the greatest treasure of all in this house."

Gerard's eyes welled up with tears. "Thank you, Miss Tivoli. That means more to me than you'll ever know."

That night, Tivoli couldn't sleep. She did not enter Martha's World the next day, but a day later, she walked through and had to repair the meadow and the path before she could go through to the village.

Evvy and Morris came toward her, arms linked. Their broad smiles faded when they saw the grave look on her face.

"Let's sit here, Evvy," Tivoli said with authority in her voice. "I have to tell you something, and you're not going to like it."

They chose a round table by the café and pulled up bentwood chairs. Morris signaled the waiter.

Tivoli waited until they had been served their ginger ales. "Evvy, Aunt Evelyn, I'm not sure who you really are, or even *if* you are, but I am grateful for all of the experiences I have had in Martha's World, and at Hickory Manor. It has been a privilege to know my Aunt, and I loved her very much."

"That's nice, Tivoli." Evvy gave her a bland smile.

Tivoli missed the Evvy that had been her aunt. This illusion, her own creation, did not seem convincing to her.

Tivoli continued. "But it's over. Barry has given me a choice: it's this world in here or the world out there."

Evvy got up, placed her hands on her hips, and stared at Tivoli. "No! You can't do that! Your great aunt has given you more than anyone has ever given to a descendant – the whole world. You would betray her just like that?"

At last, Tivoli understood beyond a doubt what she had suspected before. This was not the real Evvy; the protest was her own, Tivoli's. She spoke, as though to herself, "And I have loved it, but Barry is right. It isn't real. It never was!"

"Not real? What do you mean? Forget Barry. *That* Barry, at least. You can make him up right here. He can be anyone you want him to be. You two can live in eternal bliss and walk in your mountains, looking for his beloved rocks!"

Tivoli felt horrified, knowing that this was her own subconscious idea. Make him up? The thought made her sick, but then she realized that this is what Evelyn had done, and Cora before her, and Martha before that. They had each substituted a world, a lover, an environment that would be without conflict – predictable and blissful.

"No, Evvy. I can't do that. The real Barry is flesh and blood and gets angry and laughs too loud sometimes and even cries when he's emotional. He loves me with a passion I could never invent here! So I am saying goodbye. When I walk out of here, I'm never coming back."

"But what about me?" Evvy pleaded.

"You're not real, either. Or Morris. All is controlled by my mind, and my mind only. I'd like to wish you a good life, but even that's not possible."

She turned around and walked away, Evvy's voice plaintive in her ears. "Please! Don't do this! Don't destroy us!"

With an aching heart, Tivoli walked to the paddock. Natasha and Stallion met her at the fence, and she stroked their noses. She lay her head against Natasha's neck and sobbed, hugging the faithful, placid horse. This was the hardest of all, and she let the tears spill onto the soft coat of her loving friend. In a week, the horses, like everything else, would be gone, too.

With deep sadness, she walked up to the wall, put her hand on the hub to open it, and stepped outside for the last time.

Feeling exhausted, she walked to the kitchen and sat down. "I did it, Gerard. I walked away from Martha's World, and I'm not going back."

Gerard filled the teakettle with water and placed it on a burner. "I'm proud of you, Miss. I know you will not regret your decision."

"I feel terrible about doing this to Evvy, but, after all, she's not the *real* Evelyn.

"And I made another decision. I do not want to own Hickory Manor, so I'm giving it to you. You can stay here, take care of it, and fix up the place any way you wish. I'll do the necessary paper work."

Gerard sat down and placed his hand on hers. "Oh, Miss Tivoli. That is kind and generous of you, but it won't work."

"Of course it will work, Gerard. Why wouldn't it?"

"Have you never wondered why I am always the same?"

"Well, yes, everybody has wondered about that. But I didn't want to think about it. So many things about this place are, well, different, and I just took it all for granted, including the Gerard who is rather old, but never changes."

Gerard cleared his throat. "I knew Miss Cora O'Leary and Miss Martha Jackson before her."

"Martha?" Tivoli blinked, confused. "Everyone says you've been around a long time but..." She shook her head. "How could you have known Miss Martha?"

"It is time you knew about me, and why you cannot give me Hickory Manor. Because, you see, I'm not real, either. More real than that world in there, but still, I am also an illusion."

The tea kettle whistled, and Gerard got up. Tivoli sat, stunned, and watched as he poured water into the tea pot.

"Miss Martha created me behind that painting many years ago and brought me into her real world, so I could take care of her. It was her most difficult accomplishment, but she was persistent, and she made it work."

"But that's impossible!"

"Of course it is. Most things about Hickory Manor are impossible. After a year of Martha's experimenting, making me more and more human, I had enough of a mind to function on my own and make my own decisions. But I am limited in my freedom as a human."

'What do you mean?"

Gerard poured tea into two cups. "I have always been dependent on daily contact with Martha, Cora, Evelyn, and now you. If you were to leave, then in ten days, like Martha's World, I would no longer exist."

Tivoli stifled a sob. "Oh no! That's awful! I'll explain to Barry. I know he'll understand that I must stay here – must maintain Hickory Manor."

"If you do, you'll risk losing him. Be free, Miss Tivoli. Give up Hickory Manor."

"But I can't leave. I can't let that happen to you!" Tivoli put her head on the table and cried.

She felt a gentle hand on her head. "Tivoli, Tivoli. Of course you can leave. You must!"

"But you'll be..."

"Gone, yes. But I've been around for 160 years. How many people can say that? Frankly, my life has become a bit repetitious. It's time to let go."

"The furniture, Gerard. What's going to happen if you're not there to protect and take care of it?"

Gerard smiled. The face Tivoli loved crinkled up at the corners of his eyes, as if he were about to tell a big joke. "Have you ever wondered where that all comes from? None of your aunts could afford that collection. They are, many of them, priceless, as you know."

"Well, of course, I've wondered about it. But I figured you must have money of your own. But now that I know that you are an illusion.... Anyway, it's all so beautiful. I can't leave that. It would be a dishonor to you."

"Yes, they are wonderful pieces. Can you guess why?"

Tivoli stared at him, and understood. The realization hit her like a freight train colliding with a truck.

"Illusions, Gerard! They're all illusions! And you made them up from those books!"

Gerard re-filled the cups. "Yes, Miss Tivoli. They are about as real as I am. When you leave, they, too, will disappear."

Tivoli leaned her head on her hands and looked into Gerard's sad-merry eyes. "Everything, gone! All those years – Evelyn, Cora, Martha – like a puff of smoke, like it never happened."

"Well, not totally everything. Hickory Manor will still be here. Tired, sagging, dingy, depressing Hickory Manor will stand like an eyesore. Or you could get a demolition crew – a good one, because she will be a stubborn old hulk to destroy – to clear the land and build a beautiful little house without any ghosts, for you and your Barry and your children."

Tivoli heaved a deep sigh. "I'm sad about the furniture, and Aunt Evelyn, but I feel terrible about leaving you and never seeing you again, Gerard. You have taught me so much."

"That's enough reward for me, Miss. This is how I will live on. Your skill in repairing and refinishing furniture and your knowledge of styles could land you a very good job anywhere. That is my legacy that will live on in you – or, at least, part of my legacy."

"Part? And what is the other?"

Gerard hesitated, looking down. "Of all the women who have lived in this house, you were the only one who has treated me with more than just courtesy."

"Courtesy, Gerard? But I love you! You are my best friend, besides Barry. When you're gone, I will feel a huge hole in my heart."

"Thank you, Miss. I know that. Because of the love and friendship you have given me these past years, my existence has been worthwhile. I can go with the comfort that my presence meant something more than just taking care of three self-centered, slightly-crazy women."

Tivoli got up. "I have to go, Gerard, but I'll be back tomorrow."

The next day, she asked Barry to take her to Hickory Manor and pick her up after an hour. She had told him briefly about her conversation with Gerard.

Barry grasped her hand. "Knowing you are connected to that place in any way makes my skin crawl. I know you'll miss Gerard. He's a nice guy. But he's like that whole spooky place. Not real."

Tivoli walked slowly up the driveway to the house, drinking in the fragrance of a new crop of lavender. The brilliant blue sky accentuated the contrast with the gloomy, grimy building. She lifted the knocker, as she had so many times in the past, and let it fall. Gerard answered with his usual sunny smile.

"Good afternoon, Miss Tivoli. I'm glad to see you! Make yourself comfortable, while I put on water for tea."

"Thank you, Gerard. But first, I want to wander through the house one more time."

She walked to the heavy door that opened into the sitting room and went inside. It looked more friendly and inviting. She had taken down the heavy drapes and aired out Aunt Evelyn's quarters. The dried and dusty tufts of lavender had been discarded, and vases of fresh purple clusters sweetened the air.

She stared a long time at the painting. Every inch she knew by heart. It was as familiar to her as her face in the mirror. She felt the chain with the lock around her neck and pulled it out, looking at the tiny key. Should she go in? No. She had left for good. Now, three days later, it would be quite unstable.

"Goodbye, Evvy," she whispered. "And Morris. And Stallion. And goodbye, Natasha." She leaned against the painting and wept.

Sadly, she took leave of the familiar room and headed for the rest of the house, where she once more touched pieces of furniture, each with a history that she could recite by heart.

When she entered the kitchen, the aroma of scones met her, Gerard stood by the stove and his personal teapot was already on the table in the breakfast nook. Tivoli put her arms around Gerard and sobbed into his shoulder. "I'm so sorry, Gerard!"

"I know, Miss Tivoli. But you've made the right decision. I want you to have a wonderfully happy life with your Barry."

She stepped back and, laying her hands on his arms, she looked into his face. "Are you afraid, Gerard?"

Gerard's eyes welled with tears. "That's a thoughtful, caring question. And yes, I am, a little. If there were just an easier way. I don't mind not existing. I just don't know what it will feel like to fade away."

"You will not fade. Not for me!" She smiled through her tears. "Thank you, dear friend, for everything."

She walked out of the house, and Gerard closed the door behind her. Along the drive, she reached down and picked a half dozen sprigs of lavender. Burying her tear-streaked face in the fragrance, she walked slowly and opened the car door.

"Well?" said Barry, studying her puffy eyes.

"I've left it all behind." She shut the door and he held her in his arms.

He looked at the lavender in her lap. "*All* of it?"

She thought about the three aunts and their perfect worlds: their perfect lovers, their placid, predictable lives, full of make-believe adventures. Wistfully, she reflected back to the virtual rock climbs and cavern recesses with priceless gems and spectacular views that she had designed for Barry. Strains of the music she had created for the orchestra sang in her mind. She recalled skiing near the village with its half-timbered houses and her jaunts with Natasha along the shore. She would miss the cabin.

Out here, in this world, were real rocks to hurdle, bad falls, disappointments, misunderstandings, boredom. But also spontaneous joys, unpredictable humor, great passion. There would be illnesses and dangers that could never be predicted, babies to bring into the world, jobs and vacations that lasted all too few weeks. Life.

Tivoli rolled down the car window and pressed the stalks to her face, her tears dropping on the purple blooms – then tossed out the sprigs of lavender.

She smiled at Barry. "Yes, all."

ABOUT THE AUTHOR

Annemarieke Tazelaar was born in the Netherlands, where she and her family survived World War II. She taught English in Washington State and at an Army base in Frankfurt, Germany. She was a finalist in the 2011 Amazon Breakthrough Novel Contest, for her novel, *The Apple Eater*, based on her experiences during the war years. She also has several articles published in the *Cup of Comfort* series and in *The Rocking Chair Reader*.

Made in the USA
Charleston, SC
25 November 2012